Outside Beauty

OTHER BOOKS BY

Cynthia Kadohata

Kira-Kira

Weedflower

Cracker! The Best Dog in Vietnam

Cynthia Kadohata

Atheneum Books for Young Readers
NEW YORK LONDON TORONTO SYDNEY

ACKNOWLEDGMENT

With thanks to Gale School Elementary pals
Amy and Chris.
From age nine to ninety,
some friends are forever!

Atheneum Books for Young Readers • An imprint of Simon & Schuster Children's Publishing Division • 1230 Avenue of the Americas, New York, New York 10020 • This book is a work of fiction. Any references to historical events, real people, or real locales are used fictitiously. Other names, characters, places, and incidents are products of the author's imagination, and any resemblance to actual events or locales or persons, living or dead, is entirely coincidental. • For information about special discounts for bulk purchases, please contact Simon & Schuster Special Sales at 1-866-506-1949 or business@simonandschuster.com. • The Simon & Schuster Speakers Bureau can bring authors to your live event. For more information or to book an event, contact the Simon & Schuster Speakers Bureau at 1-866-248-3049 or visit our website at www.simonspeakers.com. • Also available in a hardcover edition. • Book design by Mike Rosamilia • The text for this book is set in MrsEaves. • Manufactured in the United States of America • First paperback edition December 2009 • 10 9 8 7 6 5 4 3 2 1 • The Library of Congress has cataloged the hardcover edition as follows: • Kadohata, Cynthia • Outside beauty/Cynthia Kadohata.—1st ed. • p. cm. • Summary: Thirteen-year-old Shelby and her three sisters must go to live with their respective fathers while their mother, who has trained them to rely on their looks, recovers from a car accident that scarred her face. • ISBN 978-0-689-86575-6 (hc) [1. Sisters—Fiction. 2. Fathers and daughters—Fiction. 3. Mothers and daughters—Fiction. 4. Custody of children—Fiction. 5. Beauty, Personal—Fiction.] I. Title. • PZ7.K1166Out 2008 • [Fic]—dc22 • 2007039711 • ISBN 978-1-4169-9818-1 (pbk) • ISBN 978-1-4169-9819-8 (eBook)

For the guys:

Sammy

George

Stan

Zach

and

Dad

chapter one

"PLEASE?" MY LITTLE SISTER SAID. "Pleeeeease? Let me push you in the shopping cart. I promise you won't fall."

"*No*," I said. Maddie was one of those kids with big, persuasive eyes, like a doll's. But a couple of boys from school happened to be across the alley, and I didn't want them seeing me in a shopping cart. I wasn't wearing my glasses because I wanted to look cute.

"Pleeeease?" Maddie said.

"Oh, all right." Those boys didn't like me anyway. I climbed into the cart and watched Maddie's face brighten, then scrunch up with the concentrated effort of pushing me. She started running, her face alight, but suddenly the cart came to a halt and the next thing I knew, my head thumped on the sidewalk and the shopping cart crashed against my nose.

"Ow! You said I wouldn't fall!"

"I'm sorry, I'm sorry! There was a huge crack in the ground." Maddie helped me get the cart off. "Your nose is bleeding."

"Yours would be too." But I wasn't too hurt to glance at the boys. They hadn't made a move to help. Instead, they were watching and laughing. As my mother liked to say, "Some men just have no manners." I rose unsteadily to my feet and swiped the back of my hand under my nose to wipe away the blood.

Maddie was near to crying. "I'm sorry."

"You almost gave me a concussion!" I said. I stomped away. I tasted blood. I knew Maddie was following because I could hear her behind me, repeating that she was sorry.

We went home the back way and stepped into the usual commotion—we didn't have much downtime at home. At the front door someone was pounding. My sisters Marilyn and Lakey pressed against the door. "It's Pierre!" said Marilyn urgently. "Why is your nose bleeding?"

"Hi," said Lakey. "Your nose is bleeding."

"Where's Mom?" I said.

"Getting dressed," Marilyn said. "You should do something with that nose, Shelby."

"My eye hurts too," I said.

"It's all red," Marilyn said. "I think you're on your way to a shiner. It's swelling."

The pounding grew louder. From the other side of the door Pierre shouted, "I'm pounding my head! It's my head you hear! I'm killing myself!"

Marilyn and Lakey kept pressing against the door as if they and not the dead bolt were holding it closed. My heart beat hard inside of me, and I could feel my face grow hot with fear and excitement. The door shivered every time Pierre pounded his head.

"Let's open it and see what happens!" Maddie cried out. Her short hair was mussed as usual, shooting out every which way.

We all turned to Marilyn. She shook her head no. "That's just looking for trouble." She thought some more. "Not that trouble isn't fun sometimes. But Mom said not to open it. Are you *okay*, Shelby?"

"Yeah," I said.

"I can hear you in there!" Pierre shouted. He said "th" like "z." He continued to pound. "I am killing myself!"

If we were anyone else, the neighbors probably would have called the police by now. But we were who we were. My mother walked calmly out of her bedroom, and we girls split apart like the sea as she said imperiously to the door, "Believe you me, no man ever committed suicide by pounding his head against a door!" She turned to me. "Bathroom. Come. Now."

She swept away, all of us following. She was overdressed as usual. Who else would wear a red silk dress and full makeup for a man on the other side of a door? The four of us formed a semicircle around her in the bathroom. She leaned toward me, examining my face. "Hmmm . . . good. There's no injury to the eye itself, just the tissue around it. And you should be thankful that your nose isn't broken." She stood up without inquiring what had happened to me. "Shelby, you clean up your face. The rest of you start packing. We're taking a little road trip." In the background Pierre's pounding had taken on a deliberate rhythm. *Bomp!* One, two. *Bomp!* One, two. *Bomp!*

To Maddie, Mom said, "Your hair—you look like Sid Vicious." To Marilyn, she said, "Make sure the girls pack everything they need. We may be gone a couple of weeks." To Lakey: "We're going to California to see your father."

I lay on the bathroom floor holding a tissue to my nose. When my nose stopped bleeding, I checked the mirror. My eye was swollen and red. Sometimes I could kill Maddie. I hurried into the bedroom to pack. My sisters had already thrown some clothes into my bag. Pierre was still pounding, but the rhythm had slowed and the sound came from lower down, as if he were sitting now.

As we walked out the back door, mimicking our mother's silken movements, we could still hear the steady thumping. I wondered how long Pierre would continue. Mrs. Gilmore from next door and Mrs. Fedderman from below were standing on the back stairway talking, but they stopped when they saw us. We continued moving as silkily as we could when carrying two weeks' worth of baggage. "What's wrong with that girl's face?" Mrs. Fedderman called out, looking right at me.

And that's how I came to be hanging my head out the car window with a sore eye, the warm air pounding my face as we escaped Pierre and the humid Chicago summer and drove toward California and Lakey's father.

It was the summer of 1983. School was out, Sally Ride had just become the first American woman in space, and we were the four most amazing girls in the world. Our mother told us so.

I was excited. I hadn't even realized Pierre was important enough for my mother to make a move like this. He was what we thought of as one of our mother's "minor boyfriends." As opposed to, for instance, our fathers, who were "major boyfriends."

"My mother had four daughters by four different men." This is a line I had repeated many times in my life, as explanation. I loved my sisters more than I loved anyone, maybe even more than my mother. They were not just sisters to me, they were extensions of myself. It felt exactly right to be barreling down the expressway with them.

Whenever we needed to change lanes and it was a tight squeeze, Marilyn smiled at the driver in the next lane to make sure the car would let us in. She used her beauty the way my mother used hers. Marilyn was not a pretty girl such as you see every day, at the bank or in the store or in a restaurant. She possessed that rare type of beauty, like our mother's, that you saw only once in a great while and that haunted you. She was half Italian and half Japanese, and she looked vaguely Polynesian. Several times, at a Chicago Cubs game, a boy would spot her with his binoculars and seek her out from across the park. The boys would just want to meet her, maybe to touch her hand. She was second in command to our mother and was so grown up that she'd even driven us to school with our mother riding shotgun.

In the car Lakey had already started reading. Reading in a car always made me feel ill. But Lakey not only read in the car, she read in the bathtub, at the table while we ate frozen dinners, and on the sidewalk while we walked to school or the ice cream store. She was a genius, according to a test she took last year when she was seven. Lakey was conceived on a boat in Lake Michigan; thus, her name. My mother said that if we were ever out in public and she got distracted—she meant by men—Lakey was Marilyn's special charge, and Maddie was mine. Lakey was half Japanese and half Chinese.

Maddie was lucky she was so cute. At least, that's the way I saw it. She was a six-year-old troublemaker. She was born with a thin patch of hair low on her back, not far from where a tail would be. We thought this was proof that she was part animal. She was half Japanese and half Anglo, pale with heavily slanted eyes.

And me? I'm Shelby. I was almost thirteen and—I don't know—the private one. Like sometimes when I had a thought, I kept it to myself. When I cried, I did so after my sisters were asleep. Now, maybe my sisters also cried after they went to sleep, but since I was usually the last one up at night, I doubted it. I needed to debrief at the end of the day, so I liked to think before I went to sleep. I had a very clear memory and could see everybody perfectly when I closed my eyes at night. This helped me think about the day.

I wanted to grow up and be something normal with a dash of glamour, like a tour guide or a photographer.

Lakey wanted to be a lawyer, and Marilyn was going to get married when she was nineteen, so she wouldn't have to work. Maddie didn't have the slightest idea what she wanted to do someday. Maddie just wanted to laugh. She wanted to play. To have fun, like my mother always did.

My mother had briefly entertained the idea that we would be like the Partridge Family or the Jacksons: a family band. We took singing and dancing lessons and didn't much like them. Then my mother decided she wanted us all to be not only songbirds, but sex-bombs, each in her own way. She could see potential in my sisters but not me, because I wore glasses, and the contacts she once got me made it feel like dust was rubbing against my eyes. So I was always clutching at my face and crying out, "There's dust in my eye!" My mother said I was a late bloomer. I hoped that was true. I wanted so badly to be sophisticated, the way my mother wanted me to be. The way my sisters saw me? I guess they thought I talked slow, and I guess they thought I moved at my own pace, and I guess they thought these were traits I inherited from my father. And because I had a habit of seeming to change the subject while we talked, they thought my mind moved around an awful lot.

I was full-blooded Japanese and, like Maddie, was conceived in Arkansas.

Pierre, our current nemesis, was a five foot three Frenchman with a good sense of humor and a volatile nature. He was barely taller than I was, but he pumped weights, so he said he could take any of us in a fight. He said that because Maddie called him short. He used to lean his oversized head in to me and whisper things like, "Do you know why the French eat cheese?" I did know, actually, because my mother had told me: "It makes them feel sexier."

When I saw other girls living normal lives, in what one of my teachers called "a traditional nuclear family," those girls seemed to be living in a parallel universe. My mother said that many, many such universes existed side by side. They existed right here at the same time on Earth, and most people in their own universe hardly paid attention to people from the other universes. For instance, there was the basketball universe, where people thought basketball was the center of the world. And there was the college universe, the rich people's universe, and so on. "There are many universes," my mother said. "Didn't Einstein write about that?"

Every so often when my mother broke up with a boyfriend, he would fly into a rage and we would have to go on the lam. Oftentimes what the men were really angry about was how much money they had spent on her. Many of them were angrier about the money than about being broken up with. I wasn't sure which Pierre was upset about, but he sure was upset.

My mother said that Pierre had a Napoleon complex but that she didn't realize it until too late. Since he owned several shelves full of Napoleon biographies, she might have noticed his complex earlier. One of the things she told us was always to assess a situation as early and accurately as possible, since it was harder to get out of a relationship than get into it—unless, that is, you dumped the guy and perhaps infuriated or otherwise upset him. That's what happened with Pierre.

As we sped down the expressway, my sisters chatted and sang Beatles songs, but I kept my head out the window, my glasses in my lap. My mother still wanted me to try contacts again because I was getting those little marks on the sides of my nose. She thought that might tip men off to my bad eyes. "Men like perfection in a woman," she liked to say. "As if they deserved it," she sometimes added when she was in a cynical mood.

I reveled in the hard wind. My sisters were trying to sing harmony. They sounded terrible.

I started thinking about how yesterday our mother had said that Maddie's father, Mr. Bronson, was thinking of coming up to Chicago to discuss Maddie's future. I brought my head back in. I didn't see Mr. Bronson often, but it was easy for me to remember him. What I remembered most was the way he always shook his head with disdain at other people, even strangers, who he thought were ignorant. Like, once a young couple was trying to cope with a screaming toddler by asking the boy what was wrong. Mr. Bronson stood directly in front of them and shook his head back and forth. When they ignored him, he said, "There are better ways to deal with that." They pulled their child away, and Mr. Bronson shook his head again. He looked knowingly at my mother and said, "I could have helped them."

"Mom?" I said. I leaned toward the front seat. She caught my eye in the rearview mirror.

"Yes, Shelby."

"What happened with Mr. Bronson?"

I saw a flicker of worry in my mother's eyes, but other than that she didn't change expressions. Then she fluffed her hair and said, "We'll cross that bridge when we come to it." My mother was very fond of clichés. In fact, next to jewelry, clichés were just about my mother's favorite thing in the world.

"He's in back of us!" Lakey called out suddenly. "Pierre is behind us!" We girls turned around and studied the car behind us. It *was* Pierre. How had that happened?

"Maybe he does have special powers," I said. He always said he had special powers. He used to stare at light switches and say he was going to turn on the light with the power of his mind. When it didn't go on, he would say, "There, did you see? It almost worked!"

My mother stepped on the gas. She used to date a race car driver, and she could drive really well because he'd given her tips. She said she would have become a race car driver if she had a little more time. I stuck my head out the window again, the wind pounding me. I felt ecstatic. The force of the wind made me breathless. My sisters were crying out behind me, "We're losing him!"

I brought my head in to look. Pierre's car was fading into the distance. I laughed. I felt giddy as we went faster and faster, and I even felt a slight disappointment when Pierre's car disappeared for good.

We were going to Green Valley, California, where Lakey's father lived. I think Lakey's father was the only man my mother ever really loved. He was what my mother called a "manly man," her favorite kind if not for the fact that, in general, manly men didn't make any money. They did things like construction work, plumbing, carpentering, and landscaping. Lakey's father managed a deck and fencing company, and he spent most of his free time fishing, hiking, and hunting. Once, he sent us stuffed animals for gifts. That is, he sent real animals that were stuffed. Mine, sadly, had been a rabbit.

Sometimes I secretly wished my mother had loved

my father. Other times I wished Lakey's father were my father. And still other times I didn't think about the fathers at all.

For our road trip my mother put me in charge of guiding us to California. I took my responsibilities very seriously and studied my map collection even though reading it in the car made me dizzy. "Mom!" I called out. "Can we drive up to see Yellowstone?"

"What's Yellowstone, dear?"

"You know, Yellowstone."

"It sounds like some kind of diamond."

Everybody knew what Yellowstone was. "Mom, it's a national park."

"A park? Honey, we don't have time to see a park."

"How about Carson City, Nevada?"

"Now you're talking."

Maddie was in charge of watching the gas tank; Marilyn and Lakey were in charge of money, mealtimes, and motels. So in this way—as a team—we made our way across the nation.

I, however, was not good at what my mother called "baton changes." In Davenport, Iowa, I suddenly noticed something. "Mom, we have to change from I-88 to I-80."

"Just say when, Shelby. You're in charge of the map."

"The map doesn't have an inset for Davenport."

"Say when!" Marilyn and Lakey shouted.

My mother was signaling as they screamed. It was too much pressure! I couldn't figure out the map. The car swooped past a sign. I turned and stared at the sign, looked at the map again. "I think that was it," I said.

"Too late," my mother said. "I'll get off at the next off-ramp."

So we lost an hour tooling through the streets of Davenport. Maddie snuggled against me when she saw I felt bad.

We finally found ourselves on I-80. A young couple stood on the side of the highway hitchhiking.

"Pick them up!" we all shouted.

"They're in love," cried Marilyn. "Aren't they cute?"

They looked like they were about twenty. My mother pulled to the side. In our car the woman sat in the man's lap, and he kept kissing her neck the whole time they rode with us. I wondered if he just kissed her neck all day, no matter what they were doing. We let them off at a truck stop to catch another ride northward. Even as the woman stuck out her thumb, her boyfriend held her with both arms.

We found a deli outside of Iowa City and bought sandwiches that were almost as tall as they were wide. We ate on a blanket in a field off the highway. The grass danced around us. It seemed like a wonderful world, where you could grow up and someone would kiss your neck all day while you hitchhiked across the cornfields.

Maddie suddenly started coughing and trying to clear her throat. "Are you okay?" I said.

She nodded, but her face grew red as she coughed. I stood up, ready to do the Heimlich if necessary. Then she blew out from her nose and expelled . . . a piece of lettuce.

"Maddie, that's gross!" we said.

Mom just shook her head. "It's beyond me how you girls are ever going to catch husbands," she said. "Let's get going."

In a few hours we came upon a series of shacks with a sign in the parking lot saying MOTEL.

"Stop here!" commanded Marilyn and Lakey. Since they were in charge of our accommodations, our mother pulled over. Such misers those girls were.

That night in the double bed the four of us shared, Maddie whispered to me, "I feel something on my feet."

"Me too," I whispered back.

We both screamed at once and jumped out of bed, Lakey and Marilyn following. I turned on the light and pulled back the sheet, and we saw a dozen black bugs scurrying for cover.

My mother took off the mask she wore to sleep better and also to hold the moisture in the delicate skin around her eyes. She squinted, even though that caused wrinkles. Sometimes my head was so filled up with all these little rules about beauty and comportment that it felt like there was no more room in my brain. "Why did you choose this place?" I asked.

"We don't tell you how to read your maps," Marilyn pointed out.

We never got into big spats, but little ones—those happened a lot. But we got over them fast. And we liked to follow a rule to always call ourselves "we" instead of "I." It was impossible to do all the time, but we tried.

chapter two

EARLY THE NEXT MORNING MY mother went out to make some phone calls, and when she returned to the room, she said she had an appointment in Des Moines. She looked at me and said, "Get us to where we have to go, my love."

So I leaned over to grab my map collection from the nightstand, but they weren't there. I pulled open the drawer. They weren't there either.

"Uh," Maddie said.

I looked at her.

She handed me a pile of soggy maps. I caught my breath. She quickly said, "I spilled. See, I had a glass of water by the bed, and when I wet my pants, well, I forgot about the water, and really, I just . . . somehow or other . . ."

She had indeed wet the bed that night, and I had gotten up to get sheets from the manager. Even though Maddie was six, every so often she still had an accident. In fact, she wet her bed once and Mr. Bronson lectured her and made her do the laundry in the middle of the night, and she was only five at the time. She'd had to stay with him for a whole week because that was his agreement with Mom. I looked at Maddie with irritation. "That's so—so Maddie-like!"

"You know I can't help it," she said, then started crying.

I pulled her to me and petted her hair. "I meant it was Maddie-like to ruin my maps, not to wet the bed." We weren't sure, but we thought Maddie wet the bed because she was such a deep sleeper that when she had to go, she just slept through it.

I unfolded the soggy Iowa map. Maddie pulled at my shirt. "Are you still mad at me? I said I was sorry."

I looked at her big eyes. "Of course I'm not mad." Maddie was frequently apologizing to someone. It was impossible to stay mad at her.

I quickly deduced that I'd need a closer view of the area to get us to the address Mom had given me, so I pulled out the phone book I'd just seen in the nightstand drawer and started hunting for a local street map. My mother wouldn't hesitate to spend thirty dollars on a tiny jar of facial cream, but city maps that would allow us to get around our destinations more easily? Out of the question. I carefully wrote directions on the paper pad in the motel room. Marilyn packed up the motel soap and one of the washcloths.

My mother stood over me as I studied the directions. She shook her head. "My sweet, hard-working Shelby. How did I ever give birth to you?" But she said it affectionately.

We checked out and got in the car. We stopped next on a street full of small office buildings and followed our mother single file as she strode up some old stairs. We entered an attorney's office and sat in the waiting room having orange juice and rice crackers while she spoke with the lawyer. I reached out to touch the plant next to me. Marilyn met my eyes.

"Fake," I whispered. Our mother had told us that fake plants were the product of a weak mind.

My mother and the lawyer had closed the door behind themselves, but the wall was made of clear glass, and the transom over the office door was open. So I had a fair idea of what the dynamics were. The lawyer was what my mother called a "proper man." Proper men were often disguised by fashionable clothes or hair, but you could recognize them by the way they stiffened when approached by unusual creatures, like my mother.

The attorney was a proper man of the bombastic, mustachioed Caucasian persuasion. We saw from a plaque on a wall near us that he was a member of Citizens for a Free Democracy, whatever that meant. I repeatedly heard him say to my mother, "I used to practice in Illinois, so I know the law there. And in my opinion you're living in a fantasy world!" I could see he was attracted to her. I knew the signs. He was trying to impress her with loudness, which he thought made him appear strong. I saw sweat breaking out on his forehead as my mother crossed and uncrossed her legs. It seemed that whenever he couldn't think what to say because he was nervous, he repeated, "You're living in a fantasy world." The lawyer actually reminded me of Mr. Bronson, except Mr. Bronson wasn't a lawyer. He *was* a proper man of the bombastic, mustachioed Caucasian persuasion. It was odd. It was like my mother was talking to Mr. Bronson's twin.

"Do you owe him money?" the lawyer bellowed. "If you do, you're living in a fantasy world!"

"I do not owe him anything."

"You said he loaned you money!"

"I said he loaned me money on an indefinite payback schedule," said my mother.

I drank some orange juice out of the container. Marilyn shook her head at me and sighed, the spitting image of my mother.

"Don't glug it, dear," Marilyn said. She took a tissue out of her purse—and primly wiped off the area right under my nose.

My mother and the lawyer turned. Their eyes lingered on Maddie. Then they began to talk very softly. We stayed still, but now I couldn't hear what was being said. Maybe Maddie's father was why we were leaving Chicago, not Pierre. Or maybe we were running from both. Or maybe we were running *to* Lakey's father. Running toward men, running away from them, reeling them in, pushing them away. For my mother, all of life revolved around men—or rather, all of life revolved around making men revolve around *her*.

When my mother was leaving the office, she stopped in the doorway. The lawyer had turned to some papers on his desk, pretending he had already started working. My mother cleared her throat, and he looked up. "Brains must have been in short supply the year you were born. As such, you are no intellectual!" she said.

She'd told him that for our benefit. "Don't ever let anyone push you around," she always told us. "And I can guarantee you, people will try." We stomped out of the office, following our mother's lead, and got back in the car.

"What did you talk to that lawyer about?" I asked.

"Curiosity killed the cat," was all she said.

In addition to my map responsibilities that day, I kept a lookout for Maddie's father. Sometimes we called him Mr. KIA, for Mr. Know It All.

In the car later Lakey looked up from a history book she was reading. "What law school did that man go to, Mom?"

"It was called La Verne," she said. "I don't even know if it's accredited."

"Is Harvard accredited?"

"Of course it is."

"Good," Lakey said, and we knew that she knew where she would go to law school one day.

When we were safely on the highway, I stuck my head out the window again, the wind blowing my hair into a mess. Maddie stuck her head out next to me, our cheeks touching. Maddie and I were a "we" within the larger "we" that was the four of us. I wasn't annoyed at her anymore for my black eye. In fact, I kissed her cheek and she kissed mine back. "I like you!" she shouted in my ear. Maddie always got "love" and "like" mixed up. She would say she loved a new dress but she liked her sisters.

The flatlands stretched into the distance, the sky bright blue and cloudless above it. The air smelled like nothing at all, not car exhaust or summer garbage or my mother's perfume. Nothing at all. It was perfectly fresh.

"Let's sing 'John Jacob Jingleheimer Schmidt' and 'Ninety-nine Bottles of Beer on the Wall,'" said Lakey.

Our mother said, "No, those songs drive me crazy. I can't bear it. Can't you girls think of a pretty song to sing?"

When my mother said no, she meant it. She hardly ever said no, however.

"Can we play Why?" asked Maddie. Nobody answered. I tried to make myself as inconspicuous as I could with her sitting right next to me. She did the doe-eyed thing and looked right at me. "Please, Shelby? Pleeeease?"

Rats. "Okay, one round," I said. "We're sitting in a car."

"Why?" Maddie asked.

"Because Mom wanted to."

"Why?"

"Because Pierre was pounding on the door."

"Why?"

"Because he loves her."

"Why?"

"Because . . . because she's beautiful."

"Why?"

"Because she got good genes."

"Why?"

"Because her parents must have had good genes."

"Why?"

"Because their parents had good genes."

"Why?"

"Because that's the way the, whatever, what the great power of the universe wanted."

"Why?"

"Nobody knows why. Okay, we're done."

"Can we play Thetheguh? Please please please? Just once?"

"Just once, I mean it. Uh, Mthegom's puhthegurse ihthegis ruhtheged."

"Whthegy?"

"Behthegecuhthecause shuhthegee luhthegikes ruhtheged."

"Whthegy?"

"Oh, uhtheguy huhthegate thuhthegis guhthe-game! Uhtheguy quthegit!"

She hugged me. "One more time? Please?"

"Last time was already one time. How can we have another one more time?"

She smiled widely and said, "I understood almost everything you said. Someday I'll be as good as Lakey." She sat back, satisfied. She loved to play Thetheguh. Lakey taught it to us, and it was how we talked if we didn't want anyone besides ourselves to understand what we were saying.

In Nebraska I lost I-80 in Omaha. We ended up in Waterloo, which my mother said was bad luck for Napoleon, but not necessarily for us. Lakey said authoritatively that Napoleon was a military genius who could work for days without sleep. He taught the world the art of maneuverability in war, and when the world learned its lesson, Napoleon began a descent as spectacular as his rise. Lakey was really, really smart. If she ever became president, I hoped she would give me a job.

For hours and hours outside the car window, Nebraska came and went. No offense to the state, but I did not think much of it. I was getting tired of traveling, and it was awfully flat. Plus my butt was sore from the car seat. The Sand Hills made a game attempt to rise from the flatness. All in all, however, we judged Nebraska a bust.

In Wyoming the car broke down. We walked to a phone booth, and our mother called a list of numbers for mechanics. Finally one answered. I heard my mother use her most flirtatious, manipulative voice as she cajoled him. Then she hung up with satisfaction and said, "He'll be right here with the tow truck." In a few minutes we were watching as our mother flirted with the mechanic, a young guy who lifted Maddie and Lakey together with one arm while Maddie screamed with delight and Lakey frowned just slightly, perhaps thinking of how, since we were going to see her father, it wasn't right for our mother to be flirting with this man. After the car was fixed, Mom decided that Rawlins was a good place to spend a night. Marilyn counted the money and said, "Can we sleep in the car?" We were trying to save enough so that we could play the slots in Nevada. Then the four of us could become millionaires and retire before we started working.

We'd tried the slots once when our mother was in Las Vegas. We got chased away by a man who said we were underage. But before he did that, we won two hundred dollars in quarters. That took us just a few minutes, so Lakey figured if we made two hundred in ten minutes, we could make a fortune in a week.

But we didn't keep going to Nevada. That night we sat in the mechanic's office watching TV and eating popcorn and candy, which was all a sort of bribe while our mother disappeared with the mechanic. I watched impatiently. I don't know why, but I was impatient with my mother lately. I didn't tell anyone this because our mother had always been our undisputed queen. She tutored us on everything except school.

We girls had been in training as far back as I could remember. When I was seven, our mother took Marilyn and me to the safe-deposit box where she kept her jewels. Perhaps I remember it as more grand than it was. But to me, it was splendid, and it was all appraised, the occasional phony piece parceled out to Goodwill or the Salvation Army. "Even poor women like to look nice," said my mother. "A man who gives a woman a fake diamond is not a man at all," she said. "It'll all be yours when I die, girls." She said this last in a cooing voice. At the bank I picked up the gems and weighed them in my hand. It was as if I were weighing my future. She said her collection was then worth "seventy-five." She meant $75,000 retail. She took a bracelet from my hands and turned it in the light. She gazed at Marilyn and me proudly as we leaned against each other, gaping. "You understand," she said softly. "I can tell you do." She clasped a strand of pearls around Marilyn's neck. She and Marilyn admired the pearls, which looked strangely like a gleaming noose around my sister's throat. My mother suggested we each take one item home, to spend the night with.

At home later I sat in the bathtub for an hour wearing only the bracelet. I held up my wrist to the light or laid it on my stomach and watched the diamonds glisten wetly.

And now we were somewhere in Wyoming watching television. When we got bored with TV, we went outside to lie in a field. It was a hot night. Marilyn said she liked the mechanic. "He's kind of like Larry, except younger, not as strong, not as tall, and not as nice."

"How's he *like* him, then?" I said. Lying in a field made me feel just right.

"Well, he's kind of strong, kind of tall, and kind of nice."

"Larry's real nice. He got us ice cream once," I remembered.

"He did?" said Maddie. "Me too?"

"You were in a baby carriage."

Larry was a handsome philosopher-hunter. He was the handsomest of our fathers. He'd read actual philosophy books—like, real ones. I used to figure, What did it matter where we came from and where we were going? We were *here*. I still mostly felt that way, but sometimes I also wondered about things.

We continued to lie and stare at the stars. "If Mom likes rich men so much, why did we stop here?" I said.

Marilyn shot me a look and said, "She likes other things, too."

I ignored her look and said, "Like what?"

"I'll tell you later," Marilyn said.

"But I want to know now," I said. Sometimes, lately, I felt impatient even with Marilyn. She whispered something to me, and I said, "What's F-E-X?"

She rolled her eyes, and then I got it.

"Let's twirl!" Maddie said. I looked lazily at her. She was always wanting to hold hands and twirl, but it made me dizzy. Maddie said she liked feeling dizzy. "Pleeeeeeease?" Maddie said. "Pleeeeeease?"

So I stood up, and my sisters followed. We locked hands and leaned back a bit and moved our legs as fast as we could, around and around. I couldn't help giggling. Maddie screeched excitedly. Lakey quit first, collapsing to the ground. So we all lay back. "I feel sick," Lakey said.

We heard our mother shouting, "Girls! Where are you?"

We sat up. "Here, Mom!" we shouted. She rushed over.

"Where were you?"

"Right here, Mom."

She and the mechanic stood over us. She put out her hands, and Maddie and Lakey each took one. We returned to the car.

"You girls know better. I didn't know where you were. You *know* better."

That was true and not true. We knew a lot, yet there was a lot we didn't know.

chapter three

WE LEFT THE MECHANIC'S SHOP as he watched our mother starry-eyed. I stared after him, wondering whether it was possible that anybody would ever look at me that way. I'd seen men already look at Marilyn that way, but not me. Well, there was Tommy Dime, who had actually kissed me once, which made our glasses click together. His family was originally named Dimitrious, but they changed it to Dime after they moved to America. He wore glasses even stronger than mine, but I liked him anyway.

We stayed that night in another dive, where my mother fell asleep first and I fell asleep last. I figured my mother had nothing to think about, and that's why she slept so easily. What I thought about that night was my father. See, first I thought about the bracelet Mom had worn that night, and that started me thinking about Mr. Bronson, who'd given her a bracelet that looked kind of similar, and then I thought about how Mr. Bronson always caused trouble with my mother, and then I thought about my own father. Jiro originally came from someplace called Wakayama-ken. In Japan, a *ken* was like a state. He visited me in Chicago now and then for one week, and he always said I could come stay the summer with him if I wanted, but I never wanted.

I guess I felt like my father was nice but kind of embarrassing. He had glasses even thicker than Tommy Dime's. That alone was embarrassing. And every year he bought me a dress that was nothing like what I would wear. I didn't know who would wear dresses like that, except maybe Millie Jamison from the class behind mine. Her mother made her dress like she was seventy years old. I still had last year's dress from Jiro. My mother made me put it on for my school picture. I walked around that day feeling like I was an old lady.

Anyway, in the morning we set out again. In Utah we hunkered down and sped through the Great Salt Lake Desert. We had no idea precisely where the

1950s nuclear clouds had drifted into Utah, but we kept our windows shut, as if that would protect us from ambient radiation.

In Nevada we repeatedly ran from our hot car to the air-conditioned markets, where we put nickels into the slot machines. After losing a couple of dollars, the slots got boring and we planned to roar through Carson City, stopping only at the hot baths. Unfortunately, the baths made us so sluggish, we all fell asleep and almost drowned en masse. We spent the night at yet another cheap place, this one with a cheap casino downstairs. I watched while our mother got dressed. She was not slender and not fat. She was perfectly in between. If she weighed five pounds more or less, she wouldn't have been perfect. Every day she weighed herself, and if she weighed four pounds off, she immediately adjusted her eating. Her skin wasn't oily and it wasn't dry. It was dewy. Even the skin on her arms and hands and neck seemed dewy. And she did just so much exercising and no more or no less. Every day she looked at herself in the mirror to make sure she was still perfect. When she felt one day that she was starting to look older, she changed the lightbulb. She couldn't stand the thought of getting older. She was perfect *now*.

Watching her, I suddenly felt sad. "Mom, will you stay and watch TV with us?"

She seemed surprised. "TV?"

"Yeah. There're good shows on."

She rubbed my cheek like I was the cutest thing in the world. "You are so, so dear, Shelby! I think you're my dearest daughter."

She left then. We played gin rummy, and later we sat at the window looking down at the gaudy street. Colored lights decorated all the casinos. I wondered if I would see my mother walking with her arm laced through the arm of some rich guy. Then I started thinking of Tommy Dime and the way his shoes clicked on the sidewalk.

Then I started thinking about my father again, who was way off the U-scale in terms of being Uncool. For the past ten years he'd owned a small gum factory in Arkansas. Before that he'd owned a baseball cap factory, and before that he'd returned to Japan for a few years. He'd actually made a load of money once but had lost it all when he invested everything in trying to sell gum in Pakistan. I didn't know whether I loved him, or whether he loved me, or whether I even cared that much one way or another about any of it. I asked my mother once where she met him, and she said, "At the airport. I don't know what possessed me." That told me she didn't think much of him. I didn't think much of him either, but it still hurt my feelings when she said that.

Our mother showed up at one in the morning and collapsed on her bed, exhausted. "If there's one rich man in this whole rinky-dink town, I'd like to know where he is!" she said, and fell asleep in her pretty dress.

The next day we managed to get on the highway by noon. Early in the evening when we neared Green Valley, California, we stopped to rent a motel room so that we could all shower and put on dresses. My mother wore a simple cotton sheath and no apparent underwear. The air seemed to glitter around her because she was so excited to see Larry.

We ran out of gas outside Larry's town, so we needed to call him. When we all turned to Maddie (who was in charge of our gas gauge), she giggled sheepishly and hid her face in her hands.

We stepped outside and listened to our mother's voice quiver as she said into the pay phone, "Larry? It's Helen. We've run out of gas." I could tell she was concentrating hard on not withering in the heat, as though he would be able to tell over the phone if she were less than exquisite. I could almost see her straining as she focused on being gorgeous. For instance, she fanned herself with exactly the right effort, not so hard that the fanning would make her sweat more, but not so softly that she created no breeze. She checked her mirror repeatedly, and every time she looked beautiful.

My mother looked younger than her age—"That's the single biggest advantage of Japanese blood. Are you memorizing this?"—and her skin was gold and flawless and radiated with what I can only call "invitation."

We hung on her every word. Marilyn aspired to be exactly like our mother. Even I aspired to be just like my mother, but like I said, my mother did not always have high hopes for me because in addition to wearing glasses, I liked animals, which were "totally useless," and because she and I held different views on manners. She practiced good manners—"A woman without good manners might as well be dead"—but she didn't believe manners came from the heart, like I did. To her, manners were just a way of getting another bauble. I tried to have good manners all the time, but it was hard for me because I liked to feel it in my heart first. My mother said, "Feel what you will in your heart, Shelby, but catch your men with your guile."

There were other things a woman might as well

be dead without—namely, clear eyes that could lie without blinking and that certain curve at the waist. Marilyn and I wondered just when we might develop the coveted curve. But we were both skinny girls because both of our fathers were thin.

We waited out there for an hour and a half. Three trucks stopped for us, but my mother told the drivers that her husband was coming. She wore the wedding band she put on when she wanted to ward off men.

Larry arrived at sunset in a faded yellow pickup. He was tall, muscular, and endearingly nervous. He was the least quirky of the fathers. His only quirk was that he didn't have any quirks like the other dads. When he got out of the truck, he and my mother stood for a full minute taking each other in before he leaned over and gently kissed her cheek. She flushed, and then he knelt in front of Lakey, her eyes blazing with pride that this handsome man was her father. He hugged her tight, and I thought I saw his eyes well up.

He'd brought us each a gift. Mine was a rock with a leaf imprint. Marilyn got perfume, and Lakey and Maddie got bugs suspended in amber. We stood in our sweaty dresses admiring our gifts. Then my mother threw her arms around him and they kissed underneath the disappearing evening sun. We sat down to wait. There were a couple of false alarms when we thought they were going to stop, but then they would start up again. The sun continued its descent. They stopped kissing.

Larry had brought us a five-gallon can of gas. Once he'd poured it into the tank, we set off. Lakey got to ride with him, because she was his daughter, and the rest of us tossed a coin to win the privilege of sitting in his truck too. I won. I told him I would bring my maps to help guide him. My mother said, "Shelby, he doesn't need a map. A man has natural instincts." She'd told us earlier that if she ever married him, she would leave him alone to be himself. She quoted her heroine, Mae West: "Don't marry a man to reform him—that's what reform schools are for." That was the first we'd heard of the possibility of marriage.

Lakey sat between him and me. She kept pulling on my arm and even pinching me, just because she was so excited to be with her dad.

Larry checked the rearview mirror. "I was real surprised when your mom told me she was bringing you all out," he said. "Real surprised."

"When was the last time you talked?" I asked.

"Oh, we talk every week."

"You do?" Lakey and I yelped in unison.

He drove so fast, it was like being on an amusement park ride. I instinctively hung on to the door handle. By the time we reached his house, our mother was furious at him.

"Someone needs to domesticate that man," she said with admiration.

He lived in a modest house. We all knew immediately how much money people made from their houses. That was our mother's training. But the truth is, while I loved a fancy house, I was more comfortable in a modest house. I didn't like to worry about breaking or staining anything expensive.

chapter four

THE WHOLE TIME WE STAYED with Larry, Mom dressed in jeans and T-shirts and her makeup was subdued or absent altogether. During the days, we swam in a local swimming pool while Larry went to work building a deck. He hadn't been able to get that week off. "*I'm* a working man," he said, meaning that some of the other men in my mother's life were not.

We girls liked to lie outside under the sun and keep a bucket of ice nearby to rub on ourselves. One day when the thermometer said it was ninety-three degrees, we lay on Larry's deck while our mother attended a yoga class. Marilyn got dewy while the rest of us got sweaty. Sweat stung my eyes. When we'd become nicely burnished, we put flowers in our hair and powwowed.

"I wish she would marry him," Lakey said softly. "We could live in California."

I pressed my lips together. I wanted to say, *I wish she loved my father,* though I wasn't sure whether I wished that or not. Nobody ever mentioned him except with a tone of sympathy for me.

"I wish Larry was my father," Maddie said. I patted down her hair, but it bristled back up again around the cowlick on the top of her head. She also had slight buckteeth, but our mother hadn't decided whether she would need braces or not. Mom said some girls looked cuter with buck-teeth, and we would have to wait until Maddie got older to determine whether she was one of those girls.

At least I had straight teeth. I wiggled my feet in front of the fan. My toes were all the same length. That was an imperfection. It made me look like I had fins. I closed my eyes and let the fan blow on my iced-down face. With my eyes closed, I could see my mother and Larry kissing. I saw it so clearly that it was a little like spying. Maddie pressed against me to get some air from the fan. I fantasized that

my mother was taking us to Disneyland. I'd always wanted to go there.

I smelled smoke and opened my eyes. Marilyn had lit a cigarette. Wow, that was pretty grown up. "Since when do you smoke?" I asked.

Marilyn said, "Since last week. I've been keeping it a secret. A guy gave me some Kools."

Maddie wrinkled her nose. "Mom said some men don't like smoke."

"I know," Marilyn said. "But I'll quit before I get married."

"I'll quit when I meet my husband," Maddie said.

I laughed. "You're only six, and how can you quit something you never started?"

"I'll start when I'm sixteen and quit when I'm eighteen."

"I'm not getting married until I'm old, like twenty-five," I said.

"Some women are divorced by then!" Marilyn exclaimed.

"Twenty-five!" Maddie said. "Marilyn, can I t your cigarette?"

Marilyn looked thoughtfully at her. "Just c puff," she said.

Maddie took the cigarette but didn't inhale, just blew out the smoke in what I guess she figured was a sophisticated manner. To me, she just looked like a little girl playing grown-up, but Marilyn said, "Good job, sweetie."

I didn't like to see Maddie playing grown-up. "Maddie, stop that," I said. "Give it back to Marilyn." She reluctantly handed Marilyn the cigarette.

"So why do you think we came here?" Lakey said.

None of us answered at first. Finally, I said, "Because Mom likes Larry so much and because Pierre was annoying her and because . . ." I lowered my voice for no reason. "And because Mr. Bronson is bothering her about custody."

We all looked at Maddie. She said, "I don't like my father."

I didn't like her to feel that way, but I couldn't say anything because I didn't think that much of her father either. He was such a KIA he even tried to get on *Jeopardy!* but didn't make it. And once when Mr. Bronson came to our house to see Maddie, he scolded me for how short my skirt was. That made me mad. He wasn't my father and didn't have the right to scold me. But our mother said we were supposed to see the good in our fathers, because they were part of

us. That may have been true, but it wasn't our fathers who were raising us and it wasn't our fathers we wanted to be like.

That night when Larry got home from work, he brought flowers that he said were for us, and they really were. The nice thing was that when he gave us girls flowers or gifts, he really did seem to be giving them to us. Sometimes some of my mother's boyfriends brought us things, but though they were giving the presents to us, they were really giving them to impress our mother.

Another night Larry and Mom took us bowling. Usually they ate dinner out while we watched TV. The bowling alley was a huge forty-laner in the middle of nowhere. Only three of the lanes were being used.

The first game, I bowled a 24, Marilyn a 28, Lakey a 31, and Maddie a 9. My mother smiled proudly at us, as she often did. "Aren't they wonderful?" she asked Larry, and he agreed. He bowled a 200. We bowled a couple more games, with similar results, and then Larry gave us a ten-dollar bill to get change so that we could monopolize the outdated jukebox. We played "American Pie" so many times in a row that the proprietor made us sit down and threatened to take the rest of our coins away.

The four of us sat in the hard chairs in the smoky alley and watched our mother and Larry act like two people in love. I could see that the few other people in the alley noticed. Some of them watched and smiled.

I said, "Someday if they get married, do you think we'll all have the same last name?"

Maddie cuddled next to me. "I want to have the same last name as you."

I hugged her to me. Then we sat quietly, listening to the sounds of pins falling and balls rolling as our mother and Larry bowled and kissed, bowled and kissed, until two in the morning. Maddie snored lightly as she lay against me, and I stayed still so as not to bother her. My arm started tingling and then fell asleep, but I didn't move.

Finally, Larry and our mother were ready to leave. Larry carried Maddie, who could sleep through a tornado. The proprietor smiled as we walked past, then called out, "You two remind me of my husband and me when we were young!"

Outside, the trees were dark and beautiful. "Larry?" I said. "Are you happy?"

"About what?"

"Just in general."

"I guess I'm happy most of the time. Why?"

"I don't know. I feel happy right now." I liked being up at two in the morning surrounded by my family.

At home that night, my mother followed Larry into the bedroom, and later in their voices I heard how much they cared for each other. Lakey made us all pray that they would get married, and we did so.

Finally, everybody fell asleep except me. I lay there until the sun began to rise. My heart felt filled with yearning or sadness or something I didn't understand. I heard Larry getting ready for work, and I smelled coffee. I got up and walked into the kitchen in my pajamas.

"Good morning," I said.

"Good morning!" he said. "What are you doing up so early?"

"I haven't been to sleep yet."

"Are you okay?"

"I don't know," I said. "Larry?"

"Uh-huh." He sipped at his coffee.

"Do you love Mom?"

"Of course I do, sweetheart."

"Everybody calls me 'sweetie' or 'sweetheart.' I think more people call me that than my name."

"That's because you're very sweet."

"I think it's because I wear glasses."

He laughed. "That too." He drank more coffee.

"Larry?" I said.

"What's on your mind, sweetheart?"

"I don't know exactly. I was just—I felt sad or something."

He set down his cup and looked at me seriously. "About what?"

"I don't know . . . Mom can't keep, like, living like this forever, can she?"

He picked up his cup again but just looked in it as if he were reading the way the cream swirled. Then he set down his cup again. "Here's the thing. Even while you're being young, you also have to be getting old at the same time. Do you see what I mean?"

And I did. "You mean Mom's not doing that. She's not getting old."

He reached out and rubbed my cheek and smiled sadly. "She is getting older. We all are."

"But you love her?"

"Of course I do."

I looked at my funny toes. "Okay, I was just wondering." I suddenly felt really sleepy.

I went to our bedroom and lay down next to Maddie. Later I was the last one to wake up. I still smelled coffee. I went into the kitchen and found the mess my sisters had already made. They were probably all waiting for me to clean it up, because I was the tidy one. I inherited that from my mother. You'd think she'd be messy because she spent so much time being beautiful, but actually, she was neat and organized. This morning Maddie was heating something on the stove. Sugar sparkled on the counter from where she must have spilled some. She was kneeling on a stool so she could see into the pot.

"What are you making, Maddie?"

"Sugar."

"How can you make sugar out of sugar?"

"I'm making hot sugar."

"Oh. I think you're killing Larry's pot."

She thought this over. "Okay, I'll stop and clean it."

"I'll clean it," I said.

I cleaned it so that Larry wouldn't have to. He had seemed tired that morning. He needed to finish a deck by the end of the week, because the customer planned to have a soiree in his backyard that Saturday. "What's the difference between a 'soiree' and a 'party'?" we'd asked, and he said you have to dress up more for a soiree. He added sadly that our mother preferred soirees.

It was already two p.m. My mother decided to take us to a public swimming pool because she couldn't stand the heat. But when we left Larry's house to go to the swimming pool, a man ran up to us eagerly. "Helen Kimura?" he asked our mother.

"Yes?" she said.

"Thank you!" He handed her some papers. Her face darkened as she read them. I watched the man drive off. Marilyn peeked over Mom's shoulder. Our mother didn't even notice. Then, though we were in our swimsuits, she turned around and went back into the house and told us to pack.

It turned out that we had not escaped Mr. Bronson at all; the papers were from his lawyer. He must have hired an investigator to find our mother.

That made me scared. That man could follow us anywhere.

chapter five

ON OUR RIDE BACK HOME we stopped repeatedly so that our mother could make calls at pay phones across the nation. We did not know if she was calling lawyers, Maddie's father, or what. For my mother, a telephone was a well-used accessory.

As we drove somewhere in the flatlands of Nebraska, the sun behind us and the darkening sky before us, Lakey suddenly clutched our mother from behind, nearly choking her. She didn't mean to choke her, just to get her attention, but the car spun a couple of times and I heard screaming and we landed in a ditch. It was like I disappeared for a second, like I went somewhere else, and then a moment after we stopped spinning, I was back inside myself again.

"Is everyone all right?" our mother asked.

"Yes," we all answered, though my neck hurt.

Blood trickled down the side of Lakey's head. Mom leaned over the seat and wiped it away. She examined the cut on Lakey's forehead. "It's not deep," she said. "Thank goodness." Then she looked with irritation at Lakey, whose face was sheepish. "What on earth were you thinking, young lady?"

"What about *bowling*?" Lakey said.

Our mother tried to understand for a moment, then gave up. "What *about* bowling?"

"You had fun bowling with him." Lakey burst into tears.

"Oh, Lakey." Our mom took Lakey's face in her hands. Lakey climbed in front between Marilyn and Mom, and our mother held her close.

"Don't you want to marry him?" said Lakey. Mom lightly kissed Lakey's forehead several times, seducing her as she seduced her men. Her face filled with love. We all waited expectantly for her answer. Lakey's eyes filled with hope. "Are you going to marry him, Mom?"

Our mother kissed her again and spoke gently. "I have bigger fish to fry," she said.

It seemed to me that this was the wrong time for one

of Mom's clichés, but on the other hand, I didn't want to say so out loud. So while my sisters nodded wisely, I just sat there. Then we girls got out to push the car as our mother steered. When that didn't work, Lakey had to steer while our mother pushed with us. I saw Maddie's face crinkle up as she pushed as hard as she could. Just when I thought we needed to call someone to help us, the car popped forward and onto the road.

We stopped for the night at another motel. After our mother fell asleep, my sisters and I took some change from her purse and walked to a nearby pay phone. Lakey dialed her father under the glare of the booth lights. The fields beyond were black. There were no streetlights and no traffic lights. A light fog blurred the darkness and the moonless sky. Far in the distance someone appeared to be shining a flashlight on a barn surrounded by looming trees. Darkness again as the flashlight was turned off. Even the motel we were staying at had hardly any lights, just a little night-light in the office and a streetlamp near the phone booth.

"Dad?" I heard Lakey say. Her face was intent. Before she could speak, she began crying and dropped the receiver. Marilyn held her as I picked up the phone.

"Hi, it's Shelby," I said. "Lakey wanted to talk to you. I think she wanted to tell you she loves you."

"I love her," he said. "I love all of you crazy girls."

"Will you write us letters still?"

"Yes."

"Will you love us even if we're not there?"

"Yes."

"Will you love our mother?"

He hesitated, and I heard static on the phone for a moment. "That's more complicated, isn't it?" he said. His voice choked for a moment. "I'll tell you, it's hard."

I couldn't think what to say. "She had fun bowling," I said.

Then I just stood there. He didn't talk. I didn't talk. Lakey continued to cry in Marilyn's arms. Maddie pressed against me.

"What are you girls doing up?" he finally said.

"What time is it?"

"It's one a.m. out here."

"I guess it's three out here. I think so. We're in Nebraska."

The operator clicked on and asked for more money.

"Did you hear that?" I said desperately.

But there was another click, and he was gone.

My sisters and I sat outside our room. I thought, I should have given him the phone booth number so he could call us back. I thought, Other men love my mother because she's beautiful, but he loves her because underneath her glitz, she's just a person full of life, like him. He liked wild things. But our mother couldn't be contained.

When we got back to Chicago, we sat on the steps outside our apartment to powwow. Our mother was busy inside, spreading mud all over her face and body.

"How can we get them married?" Lakey said.

"Mom doesn't want to get married," Marilyn said.

Maddie said knowingly, "She has bigger fish to fry."

The air was cool for summer, almost brisk. I sat up and looked at Marilyn, "Why doesn't she want to get married?" I said.

Nobody answered at first, and then Maddie—of all people—said, "She doesn't know how." And I knew that was true.

Marilyn added, "She knows how to get married, but she doesn't know how to stay married. I think she's been married three or four times."

"I thought she was married twice," I said. "Once before we were born and once afterward."

"Well, whatever," Marilyn said. "But they must have been pretty bad, because none of the marriages lasted long. One was to an actor."

"An actor?" I said. "Like in the movies?"

Marilyn nodded. "He's not famous anymore, but he was."

"What's his name?" I said.

"Grant Tustin."

"I never heard of him."

"He starred in a Western once that made a lot of money. Mom worked as his wife's nanny and then ended up marrying him after he and his wife got divorced. Mom says never to hire a nanny prettier than you are."

"Mom had a job?" I said. I couldn't imagine it.

Lakey was gaping at Marilyn. "A job?"

"The actor was mean," Marilyn said knowingly. "Mack told me." Mack was her dad. He was named after the truck. Who names their child after a truck? "Mack saved her life. That's what he says, anyway."

chapter six

THEN OUR MOTHER LEARNED THAT Larry started seeing a woman he liked very much. He must have told Mom this on the phone, because we heard her shouting at him. She was in her bedroom at the time, and we were all just outside her door listening.

She began to spend increasing amounts of time searching for lines, and potential lines, on her face and for signs of breast, belly, and butt sinkage. "The three *B*'s of aging," as she called them. The joy went out of her man-catching. Before, she used to genuinely enjoy the company of men. She liked their money, yes, but she liked them, too. Now it was all about money. She drank more, laughed louder, and wore more makeup. The men had more money, but we liked them less. They had mean streaks. They drank too much. They insulted my mother.

By the fall she had turned thirty-five. I had turned thirteen over the summer.

Lakey was the only one who saw her father regularly, because he flew her out every two months. Around Thanksgiving she came back from California with an announcement. We were about to hold a powwow in our room when our mother came in. Her makeup was so thick, I felt kind of shocked at first. "I'm going out, girls," she said. She waited. We waited. "Lakey, how was your trip?"

"Good."

"Is your father still seeing that woman?"

Lakey blurted, "Mom, you have to marry him right away because he's engaged. They're getting married at his cabin in Colorado! Call him up. Tell him you're going to settle down!"

"I'll do no such thing. You should never show a man your eager side, if you have one, which I don't."

Marilyn agreed. "Show him you don't care. Why should you care?"

I couldn't stand it. I had to say something. "Because you love him!" I blurted out.

For a moment I thought her makeup was going to crack off and fall to the ground. Then the doorbell rang, and she walked majestically out of the room.

Larry not only got engaged, he called up Lakey and invited her to the wedding. Lakey told us she wanted to know why we weren't all invited, and he told her that it was just going to be a small ceremony. Marilyn said, "That means his fiancée didn't want us to come."

"Meanie," Maddie said.

So Lakey went off to the wedding of the man our mother loved.

On the night of the wedding I couldn't sleep, and when I got up to go to the kitchen for water, I heard a sound I'd never heard before: the sound of my mother crying. I knocked on her bedroom door, first softly and then more firmly.

"What do you want?" she said.

"It's Shelby," I said.

"What is it, sweetheart?"

"Are you okay?"

"Of course I am."

"Can I come in?"

There was a pause, and I heard the bed creak. "Don't turn on the light," she said, instead of yes.

So I opened the door to her dark room. I couldn't

even see her. I put my hands out in front of me as I walked slowly. I almost fell over when I reached her bed. I sat down on the floor.

"Mom?"

"What is it?"

"How come you didn't marry him?"

"I have no desire to marry that man."

"But why? I mean, why not?"

"Because I don't. Go to sleep, Shelby. I have a busy day tomorrow."

So I left. Lakey called the day after the wedding. She said Larry's cabin was decorated with dozens of bouquets. Lakey's new stepmother had asked her to be a bridesmaid. Lakey said she was the kind of woman our mother had once described to us—a woman who was by turns plain and beautiful, depending on lighting, her mood, and the cosmic and whimsical forces of beauty. Our mother always said it took a special man to appreciate women like that as much as they should be appreciated. They were like the weather, our mother said. You never knew when they would turn beautiful.

Lakey also said that she started crying during the ceremony. Everybody thought she was crying because she was so happy, but she was really crying because she was so sad that Larry didn't marry our mother. When Lakey got back from California, Mom asked her casually for details of the wedding, and then she never brought it up again.

That night as we lay in our beds, Lakey started sobbing. We all clamored onto her bed. "What's wrong?" Marilyn asked.

Lakey reached for a tissue and blew her nose before saying, "Larry's great-aunt told me that Mom called up Larry last week and told him she would marry him. And he said no because he was going to settle down with someone ready to settle down. Do you think it's true?"

"I don't know," I said. It made some sense. But I just couldn't imagine that anyone would ever not want to marry my mother. I knew Larry used to want to marry her. If he used to want to, and he still loved her as he'd said, why wouldn't he marry her, even if he was engaged to someone else? Shouldn't you marry someone you still love? I didn't say any of this out loud. We just sat in the dark. Finally, Lakey fell asleep, and we all got into our beds again.

Then Maddie slipped into the bed with me, and I held her like a teddy bear. She wet the bed in the middle of the night, so I got up to change the sheets.

She didn't even wake up fully. But once I'd changed the sheets, I just stared at the dark ceiling. Somehow I knew it was true that my mother had called Larry to tell him she would marry him. So I cried that night too, but unlike Lakey, I cried quietly.

Anyway, that was the end of my mother and Larry.

As for the other fathers, they were there and not there. I wrote my own father now and then, and every so often I received a brief reply. He, too, had gotten married once a while back, but he divorced eight months later. Whether or not he was married mattered not a twit to my mother.

Marilyn's father lived in a suburb of Chicago. Sometimes she didn't see Mack for weeks, and sometimes he stopped by every day. He wrote her letters all the time. Some of his letters were so long, Marilyn would never finish them. Marilyn said he wrote those letters when he was drunk. He spoke wistfully of the times we ate dinner out together, and he called us "the best family unit" he ever had. It seemed to me that it would take more than some dinners to create a family unit, but what did I know? As for Maddie's father, we didn't know for sure what was going on, so one night when our mother went out, we got to talking about it.

We were playing Crazy Eights when Marilyn said, "Do you think Mr. Bronson has sued Mom for custody or threatened to or what?"

"The only way to find out is to find those papers the guy gave her at Larry's," I said. "I'll bet they're in her filing cabinet."

"But it's locked!" Lakey said.

Maddie leaned forward and whispered, "I know where the key is."

Nobody spoke for a moment. Finally, Marilyn said, "How do you know?"

"I saw her hiding something, and then later when she was in the bathroom, I checked what she was hiding."

"You mean you could unlock the cabinet, like, right now?" I asked.

Marilyn said, "There must be interesting stuff in there, or she wouldn't lock it."

That was a good point. But I brought up another good point. "It wouldn't be nice to look in it," I said.

"She wouldn't know," Marilyn retorted.

That was a good point too, I had to admit. As a matter of fact, I thought it was an excellent point. "Why would she even lock it unless it had interesting stuff in there?" I said.

So Maddie showed us where the key was—underneath a section of torn cloth in one of Mom's jewelry boxes. Marilyn unlocked the cabinet in the small room next to our mom's bedroom, and opened the top drawer. "Letters from men alphabetized," she said. She leafed through several files before pulling one out. "Look at this! Here's a letter from Larry saying he wants to say good-bye nicely. He says he doesn't want to end with their phone conversation because that was so negative. He tells her she's beautiful." She opened the second drawer and turned to us. "The whole drawer is filled with pictures of her with men."

The rest of us leaned over Marilyn and began rifling through the pictures. The odd thing was that while it seemed to me that she knew hundreds of men, there didn't seem to be that many in the photographs. All the pictures were the same, with both my mother and the men smiling brightly. Mostly, she and the man stood with arms around each other. She even had a picture of my father. She looked so different—younger—in the picture with him. For the first time I could see how my mother was getting older. And there was a picture of Mr. Bronson as well. At first I didn't recognize him because he was smiling broadly; he looked almost silly. And he was wearing blue jeans, which I'd never seen him in. His eyes actually seemed to be twinkling, and he was looking directly into the camera. He was happy, ridiculously happy.

Marilyn put the pictures away and opened the third drawer. I looked over her shoulder. It was all legal papers. One folder was labeled HARVEY BRONSON. I pointed. "Check that one."

Marilyn gingerly pulled out the file, and we fell on it like vultures. He *was* trying to get custody of Maddie. In his custody suit he claimed our mother was unfit.

"That's why she needs money so badly now," Marilyn said. "To pay for the lawyer. Look at this attorney bill."

Maddie was scowling. "What's custody?" she asked.

"If he gets custody, he'll take you to live with him."

"What?" Maddie said. "What do you mean? Tell me!" She pulled on my sleeve. "Shelby, tell me."

"Custody means who's in charge of you," I said. "Sort of. And if he has custody, he gets to make all the decisions about you."

"But I don't like him," she said. "He's yucky." She pulled on my sleeve again. "Is anyone listening?"

"You're not going anywhere," I assured her. Then we heard a noise from the living room.

"Someone's at the door!" Lakey cried out. We sprang up as one, and Marilyn ran to put the key away while I pressed the filing cabinet lock gently into place. We rushed into the living room. My heart pounded.

Someone knocked insistently. Marilyn looked through the peephole. She whispered in my ear, "Pierre." I whispered the information in Maddie's ear, and Maddie whispered in Lakey's ear.

I tiptoed to peer out the peephole. Pierre was in a suit and holding flowers. He leaned toward the peephole, and I moved my eye quickly away. We stood gathered around the door, waiting for the pounding to start. But Pierre was calmer than last time we'd seen him. We didn't hear anything for a long time, and when I peered out again, he had gone.

Our mother still hadn't come home by the time I fell asleep later that night.

Lately, she was milking her men like cows. Her coffers grew quickly. She found a man younger than her and richer than anyone she'd ever met. He had inherited a great deal of money because his father owned eight pajama factories, and he also worked at one of the top advertising firms in Chicago. Several times that spring he came over to watch TV with us. We'd turn down the volume during the shows and turn up the volume during the commercials. He would tell us who had made what commercial and what people in the industry thought of each one. When his own commercials came on, he watched enraptured. Some of them were quite funny, actually.

Our mother delighted in showing us her baubles from him. She never showed us anything until she'd had it appraised. Diamonds were the mainstay of her collection, but she favored emeralds, and that's what her new boyfriend got her. She bought a book on gemology and gave us lessons on cut, color, and clarity. She said her collection was now "worth a hundred and fifty."

My mother and her new boyfriend drank a lot and often fought when they drank. Inevitably, when my mother and a man fought a lot, he used criticism as his main weapon. This new man began screaming at her one night while we girls were in the bedroom. "You look like a clown in that getup!" he said. "You might as well join the circus." I remembered how my mother once pointed at a picture of Marilyn Monroe late in her career. "She looks like an overweight clown," my mother had said, a hint of cruelty in her voice.

"Get out of my house," our mother now said firmly.

We sat behind our door and listened.

"I won't leave until I get what I paid for." Now I heard cruelty in this man's voice.

"Get out." Silence. Silence, silence, and more silence. My heart sank a bit, until I heard the door slam, and my heart rose. I did not want my mother letting anyone talk to her that way.

For a few weeks after that, there was no man in her life. I couldn't remember another time like this before.

Then one night in the summer, she went out with Marilyn's father. We stayed at home with a babysitter Mack knew. We didn't usually need a sitter, but some admirers of Marilyn's had tried to storm the apartment the previous day.

Mack was a minor hoodlum who owned a steak house frequented by other minor hoodlums as well as some low-level major hoodlums. At least, that's how my mother described him. We'd never been allowed to go to his restaurant. He was, as Marilyn often said, an emotional man. His favorite word was "idiot." In fact, he could barely have a conversation without calling somebody or something an idiot.

We made our babysitter play Spades at the coffee table. He was a big man who could hardly get his legs under the table. He looked mean, and something bulged under his jacket. He studied his hand as if there were money at stake. A cigarette hung from his mouth. He kept looking at us all suspiciously. Lakey—future lawyer—grilled him.

"Is that bulge a gun?" she asked excitedly. "Did you ever kill anyone?" We all leaned forward for his answer.

"Do you know what M-Y-O-B means?" he asked.

I saw Maddie thoughtfully mouth the word: *Myob . . . myob*.

"I don't think you've ever babysat before," Lakey said accusingly.

"I babysit all the time, kiddo. It's my second profession."

I set down a card.

"That ain't right, what's-yer-name, Shelly, right?"

"Shelby. What ain't right?" I asked.

"It ain't your turn.'"

"I won the last trick," I said.

He studied me suspiciously and took a drag from his cigarette and rubbed his nose. "Oh, yeah?" he said, still suspicious.

"Yeah." My sisters all glared at him.

He glanced self-consciously at Lakey. She nodded her head.

"Right," he said. "I knew that." He took another drag from his cigarette. "I never killed anyone." He spoke modestly. "But if you ever *need* anyone killed, I know someone who can take care of that."

After just two rounds he got bored and abandoned the game, claiming he needed to rest. "Babysittin's givin' me a headache."

He snored on the couch as we eagerly rifled through his pockets. Marilyn triumphantly snatched something out of a pocket. It was a hundred-dollar bill. She held it up to the lamp.

"Wowwww," we said. Our savings were all in small bills.

We heard a noise and saw several boys from Marilyn's class trying to scale the wall to see her. We roused the babysitter and ran back to the window. The sitter took a gun from a holster under his jacket, causing the four of us to scream and the boys to go slipping crazily back down. We heard one of them shout, "My ankle!" as he hobbled off down the sidewalk. Then he turned to look back at our window. "Marilyn Antonio!" he shouted. "You may think you're special because you're pretty, but you don't have a boob to your name!"

Marilyn looked a little shocked before raising her chin haughtily. "It's all in the face," she said to me. For a second she became just like my mother, and then she pulled her gum out of her mouth and stuffed it back in, just like Marilyn. My sister.

chapter seven

WE WENT TO SLEEP WITHOUT powwowing that night because there was nothing pressing we needed to discuss. I woke up when I heard the phone ringing. What time was it? It was still dark out. No one else seemed to be getting up to answer the phone, so I bounded into the kitchen.

"Hello?" I said.

"It's Mack."

"Hi, Mack. What time is it?"

"A drunken idiot ran a red light."

"Oh," I said.

And before I could get my brain to focus, he added, "No, she's not okay, so don't ask questions. You girls need to get to the hospital now. It's Cook

County Memorial. Take a taxi. Don't wake up Jerry—he doesn't have a valid license."

"What? You mean Mom was in an accident?"

"Yeah, get over here. *Now.*" The phone clicked off.

I ran back to my bedroom. "Mom's been in an accident. We have to go!" I shouted. Nobody woke up. I felt a little like I was watching myself stand in the middle of the bedroom. For a moment I doubted I'd heard Mack right. Everything seemed so peaceful. Marilyn was snoring in short snorts. I turned on the light and shouted, "Get up!"

Lakey leaped out of bed as if she'd practiced this a million times. Maddie just stared. Marilyn, who never woke up quickly, said, "Huh?"

"Mack called. He said Mom's been in an accident."

That woke Marilyn up. "Now? He said now?"

"Yes, now."

She jumped out of bed. "Is she hurt?" Marilyn said, pulling on jeans.

"He hung up on me. He said we should take a taxi to the hospital immediately."

We all dressed in a flash and ran through the living room, where our babysitter lay on the couch. We girls had a cash stash that we'd gathered in a variety of ways. Mostly, it was money our mother's boyfriends had given us over the years to buy ourselves toys and clothes. We'd saved most of the money. We had a few thousand, with more coming all the time. Maddie thought we were practically millionaires.

Marilyn told me to grab some money while she called a taxi. We had taxi numbers on the refrigerator because our mother preferred taxis to driving in the city. When I got to the phone with the money, Marilyn asked crisply, "What hospital?"

"Cook County Memorial."

She looked up the number in the yellow pages and dialed. "Hello," she said, almost flirtatiously, into the phone. "I was wondering if you could give me information on the status of a patient . . . Yes . . . Helen Kimura, K-I-M-U-R-A. I'm her daughter, and we just got a phone call from my father . . . Thank you . . . Uh-huh, okay. Thank you." She listened for what seemed like a long time. Finally, she hung up. "She's in surgery. Let's go."

We ran downstairs in our group uniform: tank tops and too-tight jeans, with sweaters tied around our waists and our backs loaded with packs containing a change of clothes in case we had to spend a while at the hospital. The taxi was already approaching. We rode through the quiet streets.

"Did the hospital tell you how bad it is?" I said.

"Severe but not critical," Marilyn said. "We can't see her yet."

Severe but not critical. We digested the words. I guessed that meant she wouldn't die. I forced myself not to think about that.

"Chicago sure gets quiet in the middle of the night," I said.

Maddie leaned against me.

"It's not critical," I told her. "That means it'll be okay."

The apartment buildings were kind of sad at this hour. It seemed as if the city were pausing from its usual bustling business of being alive, as if we girls were alive in a dead world. That was a big thought, if I say so myself, but I didn't say it out loud because I didn't know if it was an idiot big thought or not.

I quieted Maddie's ruffled hair as she leaned against me. The cabbie was one of those slightly crazed taxi drivers. Not totally nuts, just slightly crazed. He stopped twenty feet back from every intersection and burned rubber when the light changed. Every so often he smiled toothily into the rearview mirror but didn't say anything. When I gave him a 15 percent tip, he said, "Very good, very good! I'll be able to afford that new Caddy now!" and drove off laughing.

The hospital was an island of activity. The receptionist sent us to a waiting room on the third floor. When we got there, Mack was pacing back and forth, an unlit cigarette hanging from his mouth. He hurried to Marilyn and they hugged. "Is she okay?" Marilyn said.

"No, she's not okay!" he cried out. His cigarette somehow stuck to his lips as he spoke.

"The hospital said severe but not critical," Marilyn said.

"It's her face," Mack said. "And one of her beautiful arms. She's going to need steel plates in her arm to hold the bones together."

That kind of paralyzed me. I didn't even know whether I should be relieved that Mom was only "severe" or upset that she was hurt so badly. Marilyn looked upset. Lakey and Maddie just stared at Mack. I felt like I was on the edge of fainting; for a brief moment everything went dark. Then I could see again. This was the first big emergency I'd ever experienced.

Mack started crying. "Her beautiful face. I should have seen the car. But I had the green. I had the green!" As if Marilyn were the grown-up and not he, he leaned his head on hers and said it again, "I had the green."

We stayed all night in the waiting room. The chairs were hard plastic, so we tried to sleep on the carpet, but a nurse made us get up. She said, "I can't have people lying on the floor." Mack was there the whole time. Finally, around nine in the morning, we were allowed to visit our mother.

We walked hesitantly into the hospital room, Marilyn our leader. Maddie gasped when she saw Mom. She cried out, "Mama!" and ran to her.

"Careful, my clavicle is broken," Mom said, slurring her words a bit.

I held Maddie back. Then we took Marilyn's cue and betrayed little emotion as we viewed our mother's cut, bruised, bandaged left cheek and forehead, her bandaged nose, her partially shaved head, and her right arm in traction. She put her good arm up and touched the back of her hand to her forehead. "My radius and ulna are shattered," she said dramatically. "I need more skin to cover the break. The only thing holding my arm together are these bandages." She motioned to her arm. "Apparently, they discussed amputating." I took a step back in shock, and I didn't even know what the radius and ulna were. But I knew what "amputate" meant.

"Does it hurt a lot, Mom?" I asked.

"I'm on painkillers. They're clouding my mind."

Our mother liked to say that smart cookies do not betray their emotions. Marilyn was best at this. I tried hard but failed, bursting into tears. Her face!

"Shelby!" Marilyn snapped at me. To our mother, she said, "Mom, you look great. We didn't know what to expect."

Our mother was staring at me. She raised her hand to her face.

"You look a little put upon," I said quickly. "Otherwise, you do look great!"

Our mother was the great denier of all time. So our conversation was laced with talk like this:

Mom: Marilyn, you're lovely, dear, but your posture!

Marilyn: Yes, Mom.

Mom: Shelby, you're old enough to start getting your hair cut professionally.

Me: Yes, Mom.

Mom: Don't ever forget, girls, soft skin will never go out of style.

Soft skin will never go out of style. My stomach clenched

at the effort of staying calm. Finally, she checked our nails and sent us home. Was there ever a more ridiculous woman than my mother?

I turned around at the doorway. "But, Mom," I said, "where do they get the skin to put on your arm?"

"From my butt," she said. "My beautiful butt."

We left with our backpacks stuffed with toilet paper from the hospital bathrooms, because we were scared we might suffer from cash depletion in the days ahead. The nurses smiled at us and commented on how "cute" we were. We tried to smile, feeling panicked that the nurses would ask to search our backpacks.

The doctor had told Mack our mother would recover. That is, she would live, she would dance, she would use both her hands, but her arm and face would have a lot of scarring. She would have to stay in the hospital until they put the plates in, which couldn't happen until the skin around her arm was completely healed, because if she hurt her arm any further, they would have to amputate it. Every week the doctor planned to put her to sleep to remove tissue that was dying on her injured arm.

We took the El home, viewing the backs of the same buildings we'd seen from the front as we raced to the hospital in the taxi the previous night. The city was alive again.

We staggered into the house, exhausted. "Should we powwow?" Marilyn asked.

"I'm pretty tired, but okay," I said.

"All right, we'll make it short."

Maddie sat on the floor, leaned her head against her bed, and fell asleep.

"What do you think?" I asked Marilyn.

"Half her face is okay," Marilyn said. "The right half."

"But you said it's all in the face," I said.

"She'll still have half a face. Hey, how much money do we have?" Marilyn asked. "How much did you bring?"

"All of it," I said.

"All of it?!"

"It's three thousand dollars." Three thousand dollars had seemed like a lot twenty-four hours ago. Now it seemed like a pittance.

The door burst open, and our babysitter appeared, filling up the doorway. "Aren't they home yet?"

"They were in an accident," Marilyn said. "We're fine if you want to leave."

"I can't leave unless Mack says so."

"I think he forgot about you," I said.

"Figures." He looked at us suspiciously. "If I leave, you'll vouch that it was your idea?"

"Of course," Marilyn said. "We can take care of ourselves. We always do."

He left, and we just sat there for a moment. I hung a blanket over the window to dim the room, and we got in bed. I lay there for a while, thinking. Our mother had said that men cared more about your face than any other part of you. I did not know if that was true. I hoped that someday I would marry a man who cared more about my heart than any other part of me. But I didn't know if that was possible. Finally, I closed my eyes.

For the next few days we lived in our apartment with Mack's sister, Sophie, while doctors performed skin grafts on our mother. Our mother may not have run a normal household, but without her, we went completely native. A couple of days I didn't even comb my hair. Apparently, Mack was handling Mom's immediate hospital bills by selling parts of her jewelry collection, because it seemed we had no insurance. Aunt Sophie came over after work every evening around seven, but she was an exhausted woman who usually got in bed by eight. Her mustache was the heaviest I'd ever seen on a woman.

The week seemed unreal. Each day centered around our visits to the hospital. Our mother grew more depressed as the week progressed. Maddie crawled into bed with me every night, sobbing before she fell asleep while I stared at the ceiling. Her sobs felt like a big weight on my back.

About a week after our mother's accident Sophie took me aside before she got ready for bed. "Did he tell you?" she asked me. She sniffed the air repeatedly. I knew her sniffing was just a tic she had.

"He? He who?"

"Mack."

"Tell us what?"

Sophie waved her hand dismissively. "I'm not important! I shouldn't be the one to tell you."

"Tell us *what*?"

"You're going to stay with your fathers until your mother is well," she said, raising her head to sniff.

"What!" I cried. "Whose idea was this?"

"Your mother's. I talked to her myself, and she said you girls should get packed immediately."

"I can't go live with my father! I hardly know him. I mean, I see him sometimes, but only because my mother makes me."

"A girl should know her father. This is your chance to find a silver lining."

She nodded dejectedly, then went to go to sleep on the couch. She could have slept on our mother's bed, but she didn't want to. And she always went up and down the back stairs instead of the front, as if she felt she did not merit going down the front, as if having a mustache went hand in hand with a lowly opinion of yourself. Personally, I would have shaved the mustache. My mother always told us we had to maximize ourselves. I pushed that thought out of my mind to make room in my head. It got pretty crowded in there sometimes.

chapter eight

"OUR FATHERS!" MADDIE CRIED OUT during breakfast. I'd waited until morning to tell the others—I didn't want to ruin their sleep. "Our fathers?" She set her spoon down and pushed away her cereal bowl. None of us felt much like eating.

"Larry?" said Lakey, unable to disguise her hope.

"Mack?" Marilyn said. "I'm going to live with Mack?"

"I hardly even know my father," I said.

We all looked at Maddie. The area between her eyebrows had creased into a furrow. I saw that she was about to cry, so I pulled her onto my lap. "Maddie. You'll be okay. I'll be in Arkansas too. We can visit each other. We'll practically be neighbors."

Her face lit up. "Do you think?"

"Yes, Jiro can drive," I said. I had met him exactly seven times. I'd counted as I lay in bed last night, completely unable to sleep. Once had been for only an hour and a half and once for a few months when I was little and my mother was having financial problems. The other times he drove up to Chicago to see me. But the last two times I was kind of cold to him, I guess. Not cold exactly, but not warm. And every time he asked me to come visit and I'd say no, I'd feel guilty because I knew he wasn't a bad person. He wasn't as bad as Maddie's father. She had the worst father of all of us. I knew we all thought that even though we'd never said it.

Maddie's father was a high school history teacher, and he always spoke to us as if he were lecturing a class.

"I want to stay here," Maddie said. She brushed away tears with her hands.

Nobody spoke for a moment. Marilyn looked down, probably because Maddie was my responsibility. I weighed my options: Tell her the truth, or don't tell her the truth. I opted for lying. "You're going to be okay," I said. "I promise. And I'll be only six hours away." Or four or seven, whatever.

I looked at Marilyn. "It'll be over before you know

it," she said. "We'll never really live with our fathers. This is just temporary."

"Why can't we all just stay here?" Maddie said.

"Strictly speaking, we can't live here without a grown-up," I said.

Maddie sniffled a bit and said, "Marilyn's almost a grown-up."

"I only have a driver's permit, so I'm really not a grown-up yet," Marilyn said. "And I can't vote yet. I'm still considered underage."

"You seem old to me," Maddie said.

"I know, sweetie, but I'm not."

"Well, can I stay with one of your fathers?"

"Not unless Mom says so," Marilyn said.

Maddie's body seemed to almost curl up like something burning. She let out a moan that sounded like it came from a ghost, not from Maddie. I held her to me. "Maddie, the time will go so fast, you won't even notice. You'll forget all about it a year from now."

"I tell you what," Marilyn said. "We'll each ask our fathers if there's anything we can do to get you to live with one of us."

"Okay," Maddie said hopefully.

Marilyn gave us each paper, pencils, stamps, and

envelopes so we could write to one another. "We'll write letters in birth order," Marilyn said. "I'll write and send a letter to Shelby, and she can write more and send it to Lakey, who will add to it and send it to Maddie. That way all the letters will end up with Maddie. They'll be chain letters. Anyone who writes one should send it to me first, and then I'll always send it to Shelby next so we can stay in birth order. Okay, that's settled. Next on the agenda is money. We'll split what we have four ways and bring it with us." Then she dismissed our meeting so we could pack. I packed seven pairs of jeans, three sweatshirts, and four tank tops, as well as seven pairs of underwear. I felt like a zombie. I also packed for Maddie: seven pairs of jeans, three sweatshirts, four tank tops, underwear, and her favorite red hat. We finished way before Marilyn. Her personal products alone took up more space than all my luggage.

Mack was staying with us that night because, he said, he needed to make an announcement. We'd just got back from seeing our mother, who mostly slept through our visit because she was all doped up on painkillers. By eight p.m. Mack hadn't made his announcement yet. We had been tiptoeing about while Mack wrote furiously in our kitchen—his shrink made him write down his feelings. We weren't allowed to bother him while he was writing. But we had to know what his announcement was.

"You ask him," I told Marilyn. "He's your father."

We all trailed behind her while she marched into the kitchen. He looked up, annoyed. His pen had broken open while he chewed it, and blue ink covered his lips and tongue. I tried to look at his eyes instead of his blue mouth.

"What's wrong?" he said. "You know I'm busy. I got homework from my shrink. He says I need to claim some time of my own."

Marilyn took a big breath. "You said you had an announcement."

I peered at his paper and saw that he was working on something called "The Quintessence of Beauty":

> *Beauty is in the eye of the Beholder. This may sound "cliché," yet is a "deeper" concept than a person might think. What is physical beauty after all—to a Blind Man? What is human beauty—to a Dog?*

He sighed dramatically, as if the weight of the world were on his shoulders alone, as if there were no presidents or prime ministers or leaders and everything came down to him. "Lakey's father is coming out in two days. Shelby, you and Maddie are taking a plane down to Little Rock tomorrow. Your fathers are going to pick you up there and take you home, Maddie to south Arkansas and Shelby to north, or Shelby to the south and Maddie north. I forget which—your fathers will know."

"Tomorrow?" I said.

"It's all your mother's decision. I'm just the travel agent."

"Why didn't she tell us herself?" I asked.

"Because she doesn't need the aggravation," he answered.

"Is she starting the plastic surgery?" I asked.

"First the docs have to take care of her arm. Didn't somebody tell you all this?"

He paused, then looked at me and Maddie. "Your plane leaves tomorrow at twelve forty-five p.m. We'll go visit your mother before you leave."

Twelve forty-five! That was practically morning.

"Why can't we stay here with you?" I asked, wondering why I hadn't thought of this before. "We'll be really really good!"

Mack sighed. "Because I ain't your father and I got enough problems."

"Jiro isn't my family," I said.

"Who ain't your family?"

"My father!"

"Your father ain't your family? I got news for you: Your father is your family just like your sisters are."

My sisters and I lay in bed that night trying to figure out what to do.

"Let's wish that Mom gets better soon," I said.

"Okay," they all said, and we fell silent for a moment.

That wish towered over everything else we could possibly wish, so we didn't say anything else. I stared at the shadows on the ceiling from the streetlamp outside. I liked it here. We had a great life. And now we were leaving that. I felt like everything was shimmering around me and was going to dissolve into thin air.

It seemed to me that everybody agreed our mother would recover, so the fear was not about her recovery, but about what her face and arm would look like. Even my face meant a lot to me. I mean, it was my face. I couldn't imagine what life would be like if I had a different face or scars all over my face. I was already kind of shy. I wished that her face would be fine and that if it wasn't, well, that was unimaginable. My mother *was* her face.

"We could run away," said Maddie. "Does anyone want to run away?" She looked right at me, but I didn't know what to say.

"But I love my father," said Lakey.

"Maybe we could all live with Larry," I suggested.

Lakey was silent. Marilyn said, "Larry's wife wouldn't like that, but maybe we could ask him."

But I knew from Lakey's silence that she would never ask him. She wouldn't risk her security by having the rest of us stay with Larry and his new wife. I knew I would go to Benton Springs, Arkansas, and I knew I had better get used to the idea.

The next morning I had rarely felt so glum as we all sat in our bedroom in our special dresses that Mack had made us wear. They were frilly things, ridiculous dresses. The morning was already warm and humid, and the lining of my dress stuck to my underarms. Marilyn had called a brief powwow just so we could all get as much crying as possible out of our systems. So we sat there crying together.

"I love my dad, but I love you all more!" Lakey wailed.

"I can't live without you," I wailed.

"I can't imagine not sleeping in the same bedroom with you!" Marilyn wailed.

But the really odd, almost spooky thing was that Maddie didn't cry. I even asked her, "Aren't you going to cry, Maddie?"

But instead of crying, she stared at the floor like there was something on the wood she wanted to kill.

Mack opened the door without knocking. "What are you girls doing? We have to go say good-bye to your mother." He slammed the door, and we heard him walking away.

He was smoking as we headed downstairs, and even though I was walking last, I could smell the smoke all around me. Mack exploded when he saw his Cadillac sandwiched between two other cars. "What idiot parks like that!" he cried out. We got in his car, and he banged back and forth against the car in front of us and the car behind us.

A man ran up to the car and shouted, "That's my car you're banging!"

Mack cried out, "Next time leave a can opener!" And then the car was free, and he screeched forward.

Someone tooted a horn and Mack bellowed, "What do you want from me, horn blower?!"

In this fashion, listening to Mack's tirades against the other drivers on the road, we went to see our mother. When we got there, the nurses let all four of us in her room at once while Mack waited outside. I was surprised how pale my mother looked, even paler than she had the day before. And the window shade was closed. Marilyn told Mom she looked beautiful, and the words seemed to sink into my mother like water into a sponge. Her face lit up.

"Mom, I'll be visiting you every day," Marilyn said. "I'll make Mack bring me."

"Mack is being very helpful. I declare that man does love me," Mom said.

It was my turn. "Mom," I said, "you're the most beautiful woman I ever saw!"

She looked a little stricken. Then she cried out, "I'm still the most beautiful?"

I hesitated between the same two choices I always had: Tell the truth, or tell a lie. "Yes, you still are," I lied.

Then Lakey. "Mom, I'll miss you so much."

"Lakey, my sweet, I'll miss you. Of course I will!"

Lastly, Maddie. "Mom? Mommy, when will you be finished with all your surgery?"

"Maddie, it depends how it goes. But soon, honey, soon."

As usual, the hospital room smelled of disinfectant. The flat surfaces glistened, but the rug was spotted and dirty. My mother had lifted the head of the bed, so she could sit up for our visit.

I took my mother's good hand. "Are you worried?" I asked. She didn't seem worried, but how could she not be?

"I'm going to miss you girls. I hate this place. It reeks of sickness. I'm not sick. I could count on one hand the number of times I've been sick. They need to let me out of here."

"You're hurt, Mom," I said.

"I don't want to stay here any longer."

"Mom," I said. "Mom, you have to stay here. I think they like you to be more cheerful. Like you'll heal better. Why is the shade closed?"

"I asked the nurse to close it."

"It makes it seem more depressing."

"It's depressing with or without the shade open."

"Well, I'm going to open it." I pulled the curtains to the side. The street bustled below, people going about their daily lives while our own lives had turned upside down. There was an ice-cream store across the street and a rug store and a deli. And it was true that the sun seemed harsh today, seemed to wash out the colors, seemed to make the world more depressing.

"She wants it closed," Marilyn said firmly.

"Okay." I closed the shade and turned toward the bed. My mother was frowning, fingertips resting on her mouth. Her face, without makeup, looked like a little girl's. With makeup, her beauty sometimes seemed to have a subtle cruelty, but now she looked innocent. It was weird that makeup could make such a difference in her face.

She reached her hand out to mine, and I stepped next to the bed and held it. "Shelby, I've never told you this, but your father is a very good man. I trust that man. He's just a bit . . . out of touch."

"Out of touch with what?" I said.

"Well, everything," she said.

The nurse came in. "The doctor is here to talk about your surgery tomorrow." Mom squeezed my hand. "You take care of Maddie. I know you will."

And so we were off to the airport. Maddie leaned against me the whole way in Mack's car.

In the airport we walked as slowly as we could. We were still "us." All the way up to the gate, we were still "us." We stopped at the gate.

"I don't like new things!" I said. "I don't like change. I like everything to stay the same."

"How do you know what you like if you never try anything new?" Mack said.

We heard the lady from the counter say, "Final boarding call."

I almost threw up. I couldn't believe this was really going to happen. I was going away. I was leaving my perfectly happy life for an unknown life with my father, and I hardly even knew him. Maybe he wasn't even my father but my mother had told him he was. Maybe it was all a mistake, in which case nobody but my mother knew the truth. Yes, that was it! My going away was all wrong.

"You've gotta go, Shelby," Marilyn said. "Quick group hug."

The four of us hugged, and Maddie and I slung our carry-on bags over our shoulders and boarded the plane. She cried almost the whole way during the trip, saying she missed Lakey and Marilyn and she was going to miss me worst of all. I felt the same way, except about her. And then she suddenly stopped crying and seemed almost cool.

On the connecting flight Maddie started to breathe hard and fast. I put my arm over her shoulder and pulled her close. She slowed down her breathing, but her face still looked panicked. "I can't go," she said.

"You have to."

"I can't. We have to tell them to cancel the plane."

"Shhh."

A woman leaned over and said, "Planes are safer than any other type of transportation."

Maddie looked at her as if she were a ghost. Neither of us answered her at first. Then I said, "Thank you."

The plane had propellers. My mother said a plane with propellers was the sign that you were going to a rinky-dink destination. I was kind of nervous about the small plane, but I tried not to show it to Maddie. I was the grown-up now and was responsible for my little sister.

"I lost my list of phone numbers," Maddie said. She started pulling clothes out of her bag as she rummaged for the list of numbers.

"I have mine," I said. "I'll make you a new list. We'll get a pencil from the stewardess." But the person behind us had a pen, so I used that, copying down all our phone numbers. I gave it to Maddie, and that seemed to calm her.

When we landed, we had to walk down stairs that were wheeled out to our plane. The first person I saw inside the airport was my father. My heart sank at the sight of him. He wasn't even slightly exotic,

Japanese-wise. He was dressed in a green golf shirt and plaid pants. He was an embarrassment to the very idea of exoticness. He wore heavy glasses. He was balding already. I could see even Maddie was surprised by the vision of my father. On the other hand, Larry had told us about an ancient Chinese philosopher named Chuang Tzu. Chuang Tzu's heroes in his stories had names like Cripple Lip-less and Uglyface. And these heroes were superior to royalty. So I knew I shouldn't judge my father, but I did.

My father grinned widely when he saw me. The fathers . . . A low-level hoodlum, a gum manufacturer, a he-man nature guy, and an uptight history teacher, all joined by my mother's unpredictable taste.

I felt as though a little conscience imp sat on my shoulder saying, *Hug your father!* So I hugged him quickly and pushed myself away.

"You grow bigger," he said.

I didn't know if he meant I would grow bigger or I had grown bigger. Since both were true, I said, "Yes."

"Hello, Maddie," he said.

Maddie tugged my hand, and I held her to me. She started to cry again. "I'll come see you," I whispered in her ear. "Even if I have to run away."

Jiro handed me a baseball cap that read KOMATSU GUM. He fumbled with something in his pocket and pulled out a small, inexpertly wrapped gift. Maddie leaned over me as I opened it. To tell the truth, I was expecting a bracelet—my mother's training, I guess. Instead, I received a cassette of "Puff the Magic Dragon."

"You tell me once you like that song," Jiro said.

Of course, I was too old for "Puff" now, besides which it was just about the most depressing song ever written. But . . . manners, manners, manners! I forced a grateful smile and thanked him and placed the baseball cap on my head.

Jiro looked at me expectantly, and when I didn't say more, he nodded. He reminded me of one of those nearsighted Japanese men with cameras who moved in clusters throughout Chicago tourist attractions. But he was different from those men. They belonged somewhere. He didn't seem to belong anywhere on this planet. Somehow he managed to have a Southern accent and a Japanese accent at the same time. He'd lived in Benton Springs, Arkansas, for the past decade, selling gum to local stores. He called his product Gum-Bo.

He seemed sober for a moment and then said thoughtfully, "Ah, you told me you sing 'Puff the Dragon' in fourth grade." He cleared his throat. "In traditional Japan divorce, someone get custody, you don't see kids anymore again. Different in America."

"You and Mom never married, so you never got divorced," I said sulkily.

"Yes. Yes. We have it annulled."

"You mean you got married?"

"Yes, in Las Vegas, for two days. Then she stop drinking and want annulment."

They were *married*? It reminded me of the time I caught a fish, and it went over the boat and got off the hook and fell back in the water, all in about thirty seconds. But mostly what I had on my mind was my new predicament. I decided to try pleading honestly. "The thing is," I said, "since the doctors say she's going to get better, why can't we all just stay in Chicago?" I pressed my lips together to keep from crying. I didn't want to cry in front of Maddie. It would only upset her more.

He nodded his head several times in a row. "I suppose against law," he said. "No adult in your apartment. And, ahhh, I suppose plastic surgery cost many money. I suppose your mother may run out of money." He looked around and turned to Maddie and said, "Not sure what Bronson-san look like. He supposed to be here."

"You don't have to call him *san*," I said.

"Ah, Mr. Bronson."

"You don't have to call him 'mister.'"

"He's not here!" Maddie exclaimed. "I can go home with you! Hooray!" She grabbed my hand again and held tight.

I looked around and didn't see Mr. Bronson. I said hopefully to my father, "Can she come with us?"

He gazed at the nearly deserted airport and frowned. "Can't leave her here."

Maddie looked so hopeful, it just about slayed me. I said, "Maybe we should just go home. Maddie can stay with us."

Then Jiro pointed over my head. "Ah, that must be him." I turned and saw Mr. Bronson.

Maddie pinched my arm hard. "Please let me come with you!" she whispered. She grasped Jiro's hand. "Please?"

Mr. Bronson marched toward us and said, "Hello, Madeline. It's good to see you." His chin had a huge scab on it, who knew why. He leaned over for a fast hug, after which he stuck out his hand to Jiro. He gave Jiro's hand one hard shake, then stuck his hand out to me.

"Hello, sir," I said.

"Good manners," he said approvingly.

He looked at Maddie. "Ready?" he said.

"We have to get our luggage," Maddie said. She grabbed my hand and squeezed.

"How do you ask?" Mr. Bronson said.

"Please," Maddie said. She turned to me desperately. "Can you come spend the night with me?"

"She doesn't live close enough," Mr. Bronson said briskly. "I'd have to drive all the way back up to northern Arkansas." He beckoned to Maddie. "Come!" He said it as if she were a dog or a servant.

The three of us followed, Maddie and I locking eyes for a moment.

Our bags were the last two on the conveyor belt. Maddie grabbed the bag I'd packed for her. After bidding us a polite good-bye, Mr. Bronson snapped, "Madeline, come!" He started to stride off when he suddenly turned.

He shook his head sadly at me. "Walk with better posture." To Jiro, he said, "You understand what we're doing with these girls, right? It's our job to get them in shape for the future. If you have any questions, you can give me a call." He paused before continuing. "Helen never understood that we have to train them for the future. It won't be all fun and games. They're going to get hurt, like anyone does. We need to prepare them for that."

Jiro just nodded, and this time Mr. Bronson grasped Maddie by her shoulder and walked away, not turning back. Even Maddie didn't turn back at first, which surprised me. Then right before they slipped through the main exit, she gave me a quick glance. I waved, but she'd already looked away.

Jiro mumbled, "All your mother think about is training you, but why argue?"

"Are you going to call him like he said you could?"

He smiled slyly, as if we were in cahoots. "No call for help," he said.

During the drive to Jiro's, we hardly said a word to each other. But the weird thing was that instead of feeling weird that we weren't talking, I actually felt comfortable. Toward nightfall I saw the Ozarks spread out before us, clouds hovering below and offering only occasional glimpses of the valleys. A flock of crows flew around the car, surprisingly close. I turned to look at my father, but he didn't seem to notice.

He finally spoke. "Flight good?" he said.

I'd been nervous on the propeller plane, but I didn't feel like talking about it. So I just said, "It was kind of ho-hum."

He nodded and didn't talk again for an hour. It was strange that it felt normal to be driving and not talking, even though I was used to constant chatter with my sisters. I could see my life was going to be very different for a while. I already missed my sisters, and I knew this was just the beginning.

I pretended to fall asleep after that so I wouldn't have to talk to my father even if he wanted.

chapter nine

I OPENED MY EYES TO see Jiro leaning into the car and saying, "Shelby? Luggage inside." I'd fallen asleep while pretending to be asleep! I got out of the car.

My father lived in a small-frame house that in the darkness seemed to be either blue or gray. Several moths flew about the porch light. The front yard didn't look to have been mowed—ever. Fireflies flashed among the dandelions.

We went inside, and Jiro showed me the room where I would be staying. I guess years ago I'd stayed there, but I didn't much remember it. I was surprised how homey the house was inside. I had been expecting purple plaid, something my father might wear. Instead there were beautiful plants everywhere. He showed me the towels he put on the chair for me, and a bottle of shampoo he'd gotten me—apple scented. Then he left the room, closing the door gently. All I could think about was how my sisters weren't there. It felt like I was hallucinating. My sisters were *always* there. I felt lonelier than I'd ever felt in my whole life. My room was small and full of unfamiliar furniture, unfamiliar shadows, and unfamiliar scents. There were two lamps, a bureau, a bed, a desk, and two sets of golf clubs leaning against a corner. I examined an unframed photograph stuck in the mirror of the bureau. The picture was of me as a toddler at a driving range. I could remember that, actually. Jiro used to be obsessed with golf. I also saw an origami crane, and could remember how I'd sent it to my father for Christmas when I was around Maddie's age.

We had a quiet dinner of hamburger patties and rice, after which my father sat on the porch. I went to my room and started writing a letter to my sisters.

Dear Marilyn, Lakey, and Maddie,

I'm here. It feels so terrible that you're not with me. Maybe we can get together for Lakey's birthday? Or maybe we can get together for all of our birthdays, except hopefully, we won't be separated that long. Nothing much has happened yet. Maybe nothing ever happens here. Today I saw a caterpillar as thick as my big toe. I'm lonely. I wish you were here. Write back soon!

Love,
Shelby

I wrote slowly because I liked to use neat penmanship when I wrote. I sat on my bed and raised the shades. Outside was, well, it was nature. I didn't see any other houses in the darkness. In Chicago, no matter what window I looked out, there would be buildings in view. There was no lock on this bedroom door, so I changed into my pajamas in the closet. I lay in bed and pictured my bedroom at home, which I could see clearly with my eyes closed. I had a really good visual memory, if I say so myself. I was picturing my real home when I fell asleep.

The next morning I woke up with my back and hair wet because of the humidity. There was a knock at my door. A moment of silence. Then the knock came again. "Who's there?" I said. Jiro peeked into my room.

Of course. Who else would it be? I must have looked pretty hot, because he said, "This nothing. Summer bad in Arkansas. Breakfast time."

He closed the door.

I looked out my window and was shocked to see that just twenty or so feet from the house, the land suddenly sloped down—it looked almost like a cliff. And there was a goat in the yard. He met eyes with me and continued to chew on what looked like a stuffed animal. His ears stuck up and his feet looked as if they were wearing black booties.

In the distance the sun was rising over the valley. I could just make out a river. I remembered something Jiro had said or written me about a gloomy river. I wondered whether the river in view was the one he meant, though it didn't look gloomy. A couple of crows seemed to be watching me with interest from a tree.

I got dressed and wandered into the kitchen, where I was greeted with five boxes of cereal, a carton of milk, and half a grapefruit.

"What kind you like?" Jiro asked.

"Anything is fine, thank you," I said, reaching for some cornflakes.

He stood watching while I ate my cereal, finally

sitting down when I was almost finished. "You need school clothes?" he said.

"It's July," I answered.

"I mean for September."

That was the entire summer away. I didn't plan to stay here that long. "I won't be here in September."

"I think . . ." He nodded sadly.

I said stiffly, "Maybe we should wait and see?" I wished he would go to work so I could be alone to sulk.

He pushed up his glasses. "I work today. My number on refrigerator." He got up and started to leave.

"Oh." I stood up also. Though I'd just wished he would leave, now I was disappointed—or scared, or something—that I would be spending the day alone.

"Nearby if emergency," he said, smiling.

"I'm fine," I said.

He left, and I sat in his kitchen. I considered combing my hair and cleaning up a bit, but instead, I walked through his small house, stopping in his study.

Jiro's study was cramped and full of gum paraphernalia: stationery and wrappers and actual gum. I also found the telephone, apparently the only one in the house. I couldn't imagine how he lived in a house with just one telephone.

I hoped Jiro wouldn't mind if I made a long-distance call. I had memorized Maddie's new number and decided to call her. I felt tingly and excited as I dialed, but when Mr. Bronson picked up the phone, the tingles faded.

Instead of hello, Mr. Bronson said, "Harvey Bronson."

Instead of hi, I said, "It's Shelby, sir." Rats. I hadn't meant to call him "sir." But it was a habit. We were always careful with him, because our mother had told us that he thought he knew everything and people like that hated to lose face.

"Yes, Shelby, what can I do for you?"

"May I speak to Maddie?"

"She's busy. Does your father know you're making a long-distance call?"

"Yes, he gave me permission before he left for work," I lied. My heart pounded from the lie. Unlike Marilyn, who could lie shockingly easily, I got flustered when I lied, unless I was lying to make somebody feel better, which was a white lie, which didn't count and which I told pretty regularly. It was like Mr. Bronson could see through my lie because he had special powers like Pierre. "My father says it's fine. He gave me permission," I said again.

I could feel Mr. Bronson's temperature rising—I could tell that he could tell that I'd lied. "One moment. Madeline?"

It turned out that she'd been standing right there and immediately began chattering into the phone. "I knew it was you the phone didn't ring this morning and I knew the first time it rang it would be you I've been up a long time we get up when it's still dark because Mr. Bronson says it's good for you." She called her father "Mr. Bronson." "When are you going to visit me are we going back to Chicago?"

"We're not going back to Chicago yet. I just called to say hi and see how you were." There was such a long silence that I said, "Hello?"

"We're not going back yet?"

"No, but hopefully, we'll all be back before the end of summer. I don't want to go to school here."

"I miss you!"

"I miss you too, Maddie."

Suddenly, Mr. Bronson was on the line. "In the absence of my being able to personally verify permission from your father, I must insist that we hang up now." The phone clicked, and he was gone.

I sat at my desk and started my second letter to my sisters. We had assumed that at times we'd have as many as a dozen letters circulating among ourselves. The problem was that though we'd all agreed to write chain letters, I also wanted to write a special letter to Maddie. So I broke our agreement almost immediately.

Dear Maddie,

I really miss you uhthegespthegecuhthegiallthegy. (Especially!) There's a goat in the backyard and crows all over the place. And insects everywhere. It's really like living in the wild. I mean, I never lived in the wild, but I think it would be like this. The goat is really cute. I wonder if it belongs to Jiro. I'll ask him about it and then write you a new letter to tell you what he says. Is everything okay with you?

Love,
Shelby

Then, feeling guilty, I wrote another letter to all of my sisters. I stamped two envelopes and took my letters out for the mailman. Mostly what I did the rest of that first morning was watch TV. During a TV break, I did manage to put on a straw hat I found and stepped out to greet the goat, who was chewing on a stuffed panda bear.

The bear, or maybe it was the goat, smelled of urine. When I knelt down to pet the goat, he dropped the bear, grabbed my hat, and galloped off with it. I tried to chase him, but he started to scurry down the hillside—it wasn't a cliff after all. He trotted halfway down before plopping to the ground and contentedly chewing the hat. I hoped it wasn't a special hat of Jiro's.

Then music suddenly filled the air. I ran to the front yard and saw a van slowly driving down the road, ICE CREAM painted on the side. I waved the van down and bought some strawberry ice cream and returned out back to watch the goat. He'd abandoned what was left of the hat and was lying in the yard licking himself like a cat. I would have to tell Maddie more about the goat next time we talked. The goat looked directly at me from across the yard. Either I was losing my mind or he was smiling. "Hi, goat," I said. He walked up and nudged my face. He was awfully cute. *Maddie would love him,* I thought. Poor Maddie. This all stunk. It stunk for my mom. It stunk for me and Lakey and Marilyn. But it *really* stunk for Maddie. I wondered what she was doing. I hoped Mr. Bronson's yard was nice to sit in, if he even had a yard. Then I felt annoyed with him. Leave it to him to not even have a yard.

I wasn't sitting in a yard exactly. There were no

fences, and the grass was overgrown. The wind blew on my face. It was so peaceful, I closed my eyes. I had to admit that this was one beautiful hunk of land that Jiro owned, if he even owned it. Being here wouldn't be half bad if my sisters were nearby.

Inside the house I found a lot of books and took one about Arkansas out back to read. It seems Arkansas became the twenty-fifth state in 1836. Famous Arkansawans, or whatever they were called, included General MacArthur and Johnny Cash.

When Jiro returned from work, we quietly ate sandwiches together for dinner. When we finished, he said, "Cooler outside."

So I followed him to the front porch. I guessed he wanted to talk about something. To keep out the cicadas, gnats, crickets, moths, mosquitoes, and big black floor bugs, the porch was screened in. We sat, and sat, and sat. Cicadas darted about, pinging and ponging off invisible walls. Maybe Jiro didn't want to talk about anything after all. But were we just going to sit there? Finally, I asked, "Are we going to play cards or something?"

"Cards?" He stood up, looking perturbed. "I don't know if I have."

"Oh. Never mind."

He sat again. A couple of hours passed, literally. I admit it was relaxing watching the sun set over the fields. And even the screaming crickets, which originally had seemed spooky to me, now seemed cool. But I couldn't stand just sitting and not even talking. With us girls, there was always talking until we went to sleep, and even then Maddie talked in her sleep. Once when she was mumbling in bed, I said, "Maddie, what are you dreaming about?" She answered, "Bugs!" I said, "Oh, it's a nightmare?" And she exclaimed, "Bugs are our friends!"

"So what happened in Pakistan?" I asked.

Jiro knew immediately what I meant. "My partner say must be citizen of Pakistan to put name on business. He say give him money, and he run my gum business and give me huge profit. So we put business in his name, and he steal my money."

Even though my father and I weren't close, it made me mad that somebody would take advantage of the way he trusted people. "Why did you believe him?" I asked.

"I know him six year."

"My mother says sometimes a contract is a bad thing, but sometimes it's a good thing."

"Ah. Ah. Very true."

He sat quietly again, and I thought I might have

upset him. I decided not to say more, but after a while I couldn't stand the silence again.

"Do you like to live alone?" I asked.

"Not so much." He seemed embarrassed. "I send to Japan for wife. She come and very nice. But she unhappy. I think I can learn to love, but maybe she can't. So I send her home."

A crow swooped through the cicadas, cawing loudly. The blood-red horizon seemed to be almost close enough to touch. The scenery was a little overwhelming, actually, how pretty it was. Jiro suddenly looked excited and childlike. He leaned toward me.

"Nobody ever make chocolate gum," he said in an urgent tone. "Something in chocolate make gum too sticky. Stick to your teeth. But maybe onto something. I planning new formula. We may be rich."

I felt kind of touched that he said "we." But I also felt sad, not for myself, but for him, because I did not want us to be a "we." I realized he wasn't a bad sort, but I just didn't belong in Arkansas. I was a big-city girl, and I belonged with my sisters and mother in Chicago.

Still, in bed later that night, I actually felt a little better than I had in bed that morning. Under the pillow I'd put a picture of me, my sisters, and our mother. That made me feel kind of like they were right there. And I know it doesn't seem like Jiro and I had had much of a conversation, and I know nothing much happened that day, and I still couldn't wait to return home to Chicago. But I don't know. It wasn't such a bad day. A little slow, of course, but what are you going to do? It was Benton Springs, Arkansas.

chapter ten

WHEN NO LETTERS CAME FOR a week, I suspected the post office of losing my mail. Then suddenly letters were flying back and forth. Marilyn's came first.

Hello, girls,

I visited Mom in the hospital today. Dad let me drive part of the way and I only hit one thing—a garbage can. Mom's kind of depressed from worrying about what she's going to look like at the end of her surgeries. It's hard, because I can't get used to her face, and the more I tell myself not to look at her bandages, the more I do look at them, which makes her sad, which makes me sad, which makes her even sadder. I hope her scars aren't bad on her face, because if they are, I don't know if I'll be able to help staring at them. I'll try hard, though.

On a happier note, Mack's nephew came over today and was gawking at me. He was really cute, but I mean he's my relative and all. I wish he wasn't, but he is. And he's twenty-five years old! That's practically a senior citizen. I also like another boy who works in the grocery store, but I don't know what Mom would think of me dating a boxboy.

More soon! Take care, girls!!

Love,
Marilyn

That was typical Marilyn. I wrote next.

Hi, all!

Marilyn, I realize you're not going to see our letters if we all send them right down the line according to our age. So I think all the letters should end up with you and also start with you.

Jiro is not so bad. I mean, I could have had a better father, but I could have had a worse one, I guess. But if I did have a better or worse one, then I guess I wouldn't be me, so that wouldn't work out, either. I mean, I'd be a different me. I'd still be me, because who else would I be?

It's quiet here and there's nature all over. Every time I walk out the door, all I can see is nature. At first I couldn't relate to it, but now that I've been here a week, I'm getting more used to it. In fact, it's kind of cool.

Marilyn, don't stare at Mom's face! I know it's hard but you have to try.

Okay, that's it from me! I hope you're all doing okay!!!

Love,

Shelby

P.S. Wait, now that I think about it, I won't see what Maddie and Lakey add to the letters, because they'll write after me. I think we should keep sending the letters around until everybody has read them, and then send them to Maddie in the end. Or is that what we already decided and I just don't understand?

P.P.S. Jiro has the smallest TV I've ever seen. He says he hardly watches.

P.P.P.S. Marilyn, I think you should date the boxboy if you like him.

I always hoped Marilyn would date boys she liked, not boys with money or status.

Our plan to send our letters to each person in turn got messed up really quickly. It was confusing, and pretty soon we were breaking the rules all the time. A letter from Lakey was the next to arrive.

Dear M, S, and M,

It's okay so far. It's hard, though, because Larry doesn't spend as much attention on me like he used to. His wife is pregnant so I guess he'll have another child, and he is already thinking a lot about the baby and all. We went for a vacation at the cabin where he got married. Shelby, I know what you mean by saying nature is kind of cool when you get used to it. I saw a raccoon! He walked right up to me and I ran away, but still it was kind of cool.

His wife is really different from Mom. It seems weird.

Love,
LaKey

And finally, Maddie.

Dear Everybody,

Mr. Bronson told me to stop calling him Mr. Bronson. He wants me to say dad. But I don't want to say dad because it fells funny. He says I should say dad anyway so I do but it fells funny.

He wants me to make fiends but I don't see any kids around. You are my best fiends so why should I try to make more. Also I won't be here long. So if I played with someone in the neighborhood I would leave soon anyway. Does that make sense?

Love,
Maddie

P.S. I'm scared of raccoons.

So Marilyn was thinking about city boys a and I were making friends with nature. Ther denying it: I liked nature. I mean, I knew eve liked nature, but I hadn't realized I liked it. I thought much about it. But in this little town it around. Every single house had really big trees, right next to them. I couldn't remember ever se that before. The modest wood houses fit right the setting.

One morning during breakfast as Jiro an ate cereal, I asked him, "What's it like in southe Arkansas, where Maddie is?"

He shook his head sadly. "South filled with ne pine forest. Oaks cut down for timber," he said. " take you down to visit your sister."

My head shot up. "What?" I said. Milk spewed out of my mouth, and I waited for a demerit for bad manners. But no demerit came. "Really? When?"

"Ah, when. I promise I will. Not sure when."

"Can I call her and tell her?"

"You can call anytime you want, but don't tell yet. Tell when we know when."

"But can't you tell me when?" Impatience rose in me.

"I figure out and tell you soon."

When Jiro left for work, I peeked out the window and watched him go. The second his car disappeared past the curve in the road, I ran into his office and dialed Maddie. She answered the phone.

"Hello?" she said.

"Maddie!"

"Shelby!"

"What are you doing answering the phone?"

"He's at work, and Mrs. Bronson is taking a shower."

"Maddie, I'm going to come down and visit you."

"When?"

"Soon. Jiro said soon."

"Hurry! Maybe Jiro can make Mr. Bronson give me my money back. He found it and took it. Shelby, I want to go home! Please come get me. I'm so lonely! Please?"

"Okay," I said, knowing it might be impossible even as I said it. "Soon. I'll be there soon."

"Shelby?" she said. "Shelby?"

"What is it?"

"Shelby. He spanked me last night." She started

sobbing huge, hysterical sobs unlike any I'd ever heard from anyone.

"Maddie? Maddie!"

But she didn't stop sobbing, and there was nothing I could do. I couldn't hold her. I couldn't calm her wild hair. I felt sick at the thought of that man spanking my little sister. We all cried a lot—our mother said it was because we were girls. Sometimes we cried as much as we laughed. But I couldn't think of another time that I had heard Maddie truly sob.

That night as Jiro and I sat outside, I asked him whether Maddie could come live with us, and he said it was fine with him but he doubted Mr. Bronson would approve. I knew this was true. I sat quietly. The night got so windy that sitting on the porch was almost like sitting in a car with all the windows open. It was the kind of night you could wish for anything and believe that it would come true. I wished that Maddie would come to live with us. I tried to picture the wind carrying the wish through the air and sprinkling it all over Mr. Bronson.

"He spanked her!" I said angrily. I couldn't believe anyone would actually spank my Maddie. I'd never been spanked, so I couldn't even conceive of it. I would rather get spanked myself than have Maddie get spanked.

Jiro nodded sadly. He cocked his head as if he

heard a voice speaking to him. Then he shook his head. "I'll call him, but . . ." But like me, he knew he couldn't change Mr. Bronson.

The next day Jiro asked me if I'd like to go with him to service a few customers. To tell the truth, I was trying to avoid being seen in public with him. I nearly had heart failure when I saw what he was wearing: purple plaid pants with a white shirt and a purple vest. I wondered if he dressed like an insane person on purpose, but he didn't seem like he did. I think he honestly thought he looked fine. My mother said nobody wore purple except aging hippies. He wasn't an aging hippy. He was . . . he was . . . my father. On the pro side, I wouldn't see anyone I knew today, so why not go out with him on his rounds? It was something to do.

Jiro drove an old car that was about as big as a boat. He was, oddly, positively chatty, going on and on about Benton Springs. "Some of the most beautiful nature I ever see here." The nearby river really was called the Gloomy River, although Jiro said it was a cheery place. He said he would take me there for a picnic. Actually, it was part of the larger Buffalo National River. Jiro said the "gorgeous Buffalo National River" was the reason he'd ended up in Arkansas instead of Japan or Southern California, where his sister and one of his two brothers lived. It was funny to hear him use a word like "gorgeous" to describe a river. Usually, that was the word people used to describe my mother. There were several waterfalls within twenty miles of where we lived, and Jiro said that during the autumn, the fallen leaves looked like gold stars lying along the riverbank.

"How did you discover Benton Springs in the first place?" I asked.

"Student at college," he said. He smiled ruefully. "Couldn't get in anywhere else."

He was driving boxes of Gum-Bo to customers in the area. I was chewing some. Gum-Bo tasted like it had a bit of licorice in it, maybe even a bit of apple. I couldn't quite figure it out. But it was good. Really good. "What all do you put in your gum?" I asked.

He seemed surprised. "Gum maker never tell formula."

We drove to a place called the Sherwood Local Emporium. The only other buildings nearby were a small gas station and a small medical clinic that looked closed. Before we got out of the car, Jiro cautioned me, "Mrs. Sherwood have no neck."

"No neck?"

He nodded. "I know you have good manner,

but I just want warn so not surprised."

I had no idea what he was talking about, but when we walked into the emporium, I saw a woman standing at the counter. She had no neck. Her head was just planted right there on her shoulders.

Mrs. Sherwood was a small, squat woman with a happy face. I admit I was curious about how she turned her head. Did she have to turn her whole torso to look left and right? Jiro eyed me warningly.

Even though I was curious, I didn't judge Mrs. Sherwood for not having a neck. I thought again about Chuang Tzu's heroes like Cripple Lipless and Uglyface.

Jiro set his box of gum on the counter, and Mrs. Sherwood smiled widely, not at the gum, but at me. The store didn't look much different from any little store in Chicago or Nebraska or wherever. There were the usual brands of bread and soft drinks and everything else. But there was also my father's gum, prominently displayed on the counter.

Jiro said, "My daughter, Shelby."

"My husband says you mentioned once that you had a daughter! Isn't she lovely?" And she smiled as if I really was lovely.

"She play piano. Take lessons for, *anooooo*, ah . . ."

"Well, it was only four months," I mumbled.

"Isn't that wonderful?" Mrs. Sherwood said, as if it truly was wonderful. She radiated happiness. "I wish Mr. Sherwood were here so he could meet her. When my kids grew up and moved out, I never felt so proud, but it broke my heart at the same time. It's nice to have young people around, isn't it?"

"Yes," said Jiro, but I couldn't tell whether he meant it.

Mrs. Sherwood leaned toward me. "You should be very proud, because your father makes the best gum I've ever tasted. If this were a fair world, he would be as rich as the Wrigleys."

She handed my father a check, and we left.

As we drove again in his boat car, he said, "Some children make fun of Mrs. Sherwood for not having neck. I'm proud of you."

"I wouldn't make fun of someone!"

"I know. You're good girl."

Our next stop was twenty miles of scenic road away. There wasn't much along the road, just occasional clusters of frame buildings. I leaned out the window like a dog and tried to imagine gold stars lying along the highway. After a while we stopped at a place called Ark-Mart.

According to Jiro, the owner, Mr. Lumpkin, briefly "went crazy" more than a decade ago. Then he opened this store. He had studied zoology at an Ivy League school, and in his professional life he had specialized in coyotes, helping to eradicate them for the government. He later decided killing coyotes was only making them smarter in the ways of not getting killed. And he began to love the coyotes. "This is when he go crazy," Jiro said.

He chuckled. "Mr. Lumpkin say he once swallowed live fish to see if he could feel fish soul when it died."

"Could he?" I asked.

Jiro frowned as he turned off the engine outside Mr. Lumpkin's store. He seemed very deep in thought. "In Japan some people take live shrimp, cut off head and tail very quick, and swallow. They say this best way to eat shrimp and get full flavor. I try once, but I don't feel soul." He smiled at me. "Good question."

When we got out of the car, Jiro said, "You carry box." He opened the trunk and I paused. My mother probably would have been appalled: She was not raising her girls to be gum salesmen. Even though I was tidy, I had never done much work. Our mother actually hired a housekeeper when the apartment got out of hand. But Jiro was waiting patiently, so I picked up the box and followed him inside.

Mr. Lumpkin looked perfectly normal, except maybe a little stiff—he had a military haircut and his face was chiseled. I noticed about a dozen pictures of coyotes behind the counter.

The first thing Jiro said was, "My daughter, Shelby."

Mr. Lumpkin nodded, but severely, and handed Jiro a check. "Last batch didn't seem as fresh," he said.

"Very sorry," Jiro said. "This batch excellent."

Mr. Lumpkin nodded severely again, and we left.

After we'd driven a few miles, Jiro said, "Last batch very fresh, but why argue?"

We rarely passed other cars on the road. I had no idea who would actually shop at these tiny stores and buy Jiro's gum. But he seemed to be making a passable living.

Next we stopped at someplace called Farmer Pete's. Jiro walked straight to the animal feed section, picking up a sack of oats specially prepared for goats. He told the clerk that he also needed some hay. To me, he said, "Don't overfeed. Goat keep eating and eating. You need to be strong and not feed him just because he begs."

We made a few more stops before returning home to eat sandwiches and sit on the porch. I put out some hay and fresh water for my goat. He ran right up but stopped a few feet away. "Don't worry, I'm leaving," I told him. "I don't want to scare you."

I hurried to my bedroom and peeked out the window. The goat was eating the hay. It seemed to me he looked happy. Jiro knocked on the door. "I'm going back to office," he said.

"Okay, bye!" I said. I watched my goat until he finished eating and went wherever it was he went.

I always ran outside whenever the mailman came, but I didn't get a letter until a week later, when I got three from Maddie. They were just to me, not one of our chain letters.

Dear Shelby,

I dont like it here. You said you were going to vissit me. Did you tell a lie? I have to put this letter under the matress. Else my father will get it. I wet the bed last night and he spanked me again. Can you come visit me? Please? Please???

Lihthegove,
Maddie

The next two letters said pretty much the same thing. She thought I'd abandoned her. I pictured her big eyes when she wrote "please." I could see her face perfectly in my mind. The letter sounded so serious. I had a big responsibility to save her from living with Mr. Bronson. I tried sending her thoughts about how everything would be okay. I tried to think of ways that I could go get her. Maybe if our mother knew Mr. Bronson was spanking her, she would insist Maddie stay here. I called Marilyn to see what she thought, but no one picked up.

As soon as I hung up the phone, it rang. I knew it was one of my sisters, because we thought we were all psychic, so I figured that if I was thinking about them, then they were thinking about me. "Hi," I said.

"Are you going to come get me?"

"I am, Maddie," I said. "I said I would, and I'm going to. I just—"

"Who is this?" said Mr. Bronson's voice in my ear.

"It's me, Shelby."

"She doesn't have permission to call you." The phone clicked.

That evening I was so quiet that even Jiro, himself quiet, asked me if anything was wrong. I said no, and we listened to the cries of crickets and watched the sun setting over the hills. A grasshopper jumped onto the screen, and then a bird slammed into the screen before righting itself and flying away. Jiro said thousands and maybe even millions of birds were killed each year, flying into glass on skyscrapers. "You should be on *Jeopardy!*," I told him.

"What jeopardy?"

He was just like my mother asking about Yellowstone. "You don't know what *Jeopardy!* is?"

"Ah, jeopardy is when in danger. I read that in dictionary."

Was anyone ever as out of it as my father? "It's a TV game show," I said.

"Oh, TV," he said, as if that were the end of it.

Later, when I got in bed, I felt angry that Maddie wasn't even allowed to call me. I hadn't even been able to tell her anything. When I pictured Maddie wetting the bed as she dreamed about our good friends the bugs, I just wanted to kill Mr. Bronson for spanking her. In fact, I felt so angry I couldn't sleep. Then I got angrier and angrier, and when I did fall asleep, I dreamed of Mr. Bronson losing on *Jeopardy!*

chapter eleven

I CALLED MARILYN AGAIN THE next day, the second Jiro left the house.

When she answered, I said, "It's me."

"Hi, Shelby."

"Maddie says that Mr. Bronson spanked her for wetting the bed. And then she called me and he made her hang up."

"He's such a jerk. She can't help it! I can't stand him."

"Me neither. I was thinking we should ask Mom if Maddie can stay with you and Mack or me and Jiro. Then at least she'll be with one of us."

"I already asked," Marilyn told me.

"You did?"

"Uh-huh. She said she didn't want to rock the boat with Bronson at the moment because of some legal stuff."

"When did you ask? Maybe you can ask Mom again next time you see her. Tell her Mr. Bronson spanked her. Is she getting any better?"

"I see her every day. Her arm's getting better. But she's pretty depressed."

"But she's getting better."

"She looks bad," Marilyn said. And that told me everything. "Shelby, I know you're worried about Maddie, but I don't want to upset Mom. She's very emotional right now. I don't think it's a good idea to ask her something that will only worry her."

Exasperation and anger rose in me. But I also felt guilty for being mad at someone going through surgery after surgery. I wasn't sure what my mother even looked like now. Marilyn said her looks were going through a "challenging" period.

The next day Marilyn called back. She'd talked to Mom about Maddie after all. "Mom started crying and saying there was nothing she could do. She said Bronson was taking advantage of the situation."

So the days formed weeks, and still Maddie cried whenever we talked. During that time, our mother was released from the hospital once and then readmitted a few days later to have the plates put in her forearm. Meanwhile, as summer ripened, the last kousa dogwood blooms dropped from the trees in Jiro's front yard. The hillsides were all the same deep green, and at night the air was thick with mosquitoes. No matter how careful Jiro and I were about closing our screens and getting quickly into and out of the house, every night I would lie in bed and hear buzzing in my ears. Sometimes I turned on the light and went on a mosquito hunt, smashing a few mosquitoes and seeing blood squirt out.

One day I sat outside with my new goat friend and some nail polish. At first the goat was curious, maybe wondering if this new activity involved some kind of snack for him. When he saw it didn't, he walked a few feet away and folded his legs under himself and watched me.

Painted nails never helped my feet look any better. It seemed to just make my funny toes look even funnier. My feet had never been soft and pretty. In fact, they were so bad that when Maddie was a toddler, she asked me if my feet were "broken" because they were as cracked as a drought-stricken field.

They were even worse now. Since my sisters and I had always painted our nails together every week, it just made me lonely to do it now.

I went inside and got the *A* volume of Jiro's encyclopedia set. Jiro had shown it to me and said I could read it when I had nothing to do. He said he'd read the whole set from *A* to *Z*. I randomly opened up the volume and read, *Marie Antoinette is perhaps most famous for her alleged line "Let them eat cake."*

I looked at the goat. "Who cares what she said?" I said. "She lived a million years ago."

Jiro said that not only had he read the entire encyclopedia set, he'd also read two different dictionaries. Nobody read one entire dictionary, let alone two. I took a dictionary and got through one fourth of one page before I stopped. All I was able to focus on was that I couldn't wait to go back to Chicago and be with my sisters again. We had such a great time together. Without them, I didn't really seem to be living my life. It was like my life was on hold and I was living in some kind of temporary world. The only thing important to me was writing my sisters and getting mail from them. Later that day I got Maddie's next batch of letters:

Duhthegear Shelby,

I hope you are doing well. My father is helping me to write my letters. I sincerely hope you are doing well. I am doing well and am grateful to Father for helping me get through this difficult time.

Luhthegove,
Madeline

The letter struck me as really creepy. I pictured Mr. Bronson sitting next to her, okaying each sentence as she wrote. Maybe he even dictated the words to her. I ripped open the other two letters, and they were the same way. By the time Jiro got home I'd started to worry that Mr. Bronson didn't have to dictate anything to Maddie—he'd beaten her down so much, he was changing her personality. I ran up to greet my father. "It's an emergency!" I cried out, holding a letter out to him. He looked concerned when he started the letter, but not when he finished it. "Why is this emergency?" he said.

"He was dictating the letter to her!" I said.

Jiro looked confused. "How you know that?"

"It doesn't sound like her."

"Who it sound like?"

"Nobody," I said. I got a little irate with Jiro. "Nobody! That's the point."

"I have long day today. Lost account because I charge more than competitor. I can't afford to charge less."

"But . . ." But I couldn't say more. I guess I felt kind of like I had to defend Jiro from this competitor. But I also had to take care of Maddie. Why did the world give you twice as much as you could handle?

Sitting on the porch had already become a tradition. That night I sat out there before Jiro did, and he came and joined me.

"So can we have Maddie up for a visit?"

"Ahh, that would be up to Bronson-san."

"You don't have to call him *san*. Also, I was wondering, why do you keep a goat?" I asked Jiro.

"I don't keep. He just decide to live here one day."

"He's my friend."

"I know," Jiro said. "I see you out there when I get home."

"Do you think we could get him something?"

"Something?"

"I don't know. Goat treats."

"Ah, I think, ah, the oats and hay make happy goat."

"I meant a chew toy or snack."

Just then the phone rang, and I knew it was Maddie. I just got right up, went inside, picked up the phone, and said, "Hi, Maddie."

"Hi," she said. "My father let me call you tonight because I was good today."

"Is he standing right there?"

"Yes," she answered. "How are you?"

"I'm fine, how are you?"

She hesitated, then said, "Okay. Mr. Bronson, uh, Father is teaching me French."

"Mom would like that. It's very sophisticated."

"What's surfisticated?"

"Sophisticated. I can't explain what it means, but French is sophisticated. A wineglass and a diamond bracelet are probably sophisticated also."

"Oh. How interesting, Shelby!"

"Mom is sophisticated." Then I thought, *How interesting, Shelby?* Since when did Maddie say "How interesting, Shelby"?

"My father prefers not to talk about her. You know what? I have to go. My father just wanted me to call you and let you know that things are going well." I heard Mr. Bronson in the background saying something. Maddie continued, "Things are going very well. Good-bye."

"Bye, Maddie." I hung up and then stared at the phone for a second. That was a very weird conversation.

I returned to the porch. Jiro was smoking a cigar, which I'd never seen him do before and which smelled about as bad as a thing can smell. He said, "Sometimes I think maybe I should import cigar to supplement gum business. Or maybe make baseball cap again." He looked at me as if for an opinion.

"Gum and cigars?" I said. "I guess they're kind of related. You put them both in your mouth."

He nodded thoughtfully.

"Jiro?"

"Ah?"

"Why can't Maddie live here? I could go get her secretly, and I would pay for everything. I have some money. It wouldn't cost you anything."

He puffed on his cigar. "Bronson-san her father," he said firmly. "I already ask him about visit."

"Really? When did you ask? What did he say?"

"I call last week. He say no very strong. He say he

expert in raising child. He say he working on book about it."

I'm going to go get her, I thought, but all I said was, "You don't have to call him *san*. I thought you said that only when you respected someone."

"I respect everyone," he said. "Even Bronson-san."

chapter twelve

I DECIDED I WOULD HIDE Maddie in the garage. I went out and looked around the next morning. I took the broom and cleaned away the spiderwebs and swept the floor. Because I'd left the door open, the goat came in and tried to eat the straw on the broom. "No!" I said. "No!" But he didn't pay any attention to me. He grabbed the broom and pulled hard. I pulled back. "Out!" I said. For a reply, he tugged even harder. I tried to change my grip, and he took the opportunity to pull the broom away. He ran outside, and I chased him until he ran down the steep hill.

Anyway, the garage wasn't the Ritz, but it wasn't so bad. The thought of going after Maddie was scary, but I kept thinking of our mother. One thing she said over and over was, "It isn't what you decide that matters, but what you do. I think Bertrand Russell said that . . . or one of those philosophers. It doesn't matter which." I had to do something. I felt like it was my responsibility to act before Maddie's personality was squashed for life. That afternoon I got this letter from her:

Dearest Shelby,

Everything is great here. I'm having a superb time staying with my father and his wife. He'll be going to visit his brother next week, and I'll stay here with my stepmother. I hope all is well with you.

Sincerely,
Madeline

"Sincerely"? "Superb"? "Madeline"? The letter sounded like a robot wrote it—a little Bronson robot, to be more specific. I knew she wasn't having a good time. What was scaring me was that Maddie would start to think that it was normal to feel miserable the way Sophie thought that it was normal. I reread the letter several times and then pulled out the phone book. I saw that the local bus stop was right there at Mrs. Sherwood's store. I called the emporium.

"Hi. My name is Suzy," I lied.

"Suzy?"

"Yes, and I was wondering when the bus south comes through."

"Oh, you mean the bus to Little Rock?"

"I was thinking of Cortez."

"Suzy . . . Suzy . . . I don't think I know you," Mrs. Sherwood said cheerfully.

What difference did it make? But I felt panicked. "I was just asking for my cousin."

"The bus passes through at two in the morning. You can buy a ticket from me during the day or on the bus. But if you don't let me know ahead of time, you'll need to wave the bus down with a flashlight. It's a flag stop. The bus doesn't stop unless somebody's there."

I called Maddie that evening while Jiro sat outside. Mr. Bronson answered. "Hi, it's Shelby," I said. "I have permission from my father to call Maddie."

"Five minutes," he said.

"Hello?" It was Maddie. She must have been standing right there.

I lowered my voice, as if Mr. Bronson could hear me. "Maddie, I'm catching a bus tonight," I said urgently. "I'll be there by early morning to bring you here. Don't pack, or Mr. Bronson might figure out what's going on. Stay put. Just say 'okay.'"

"Okay."

"See you soon."

"Bthegye," she said excitedly, and then hung up.

That night after Jiro fell asleep, I sneaked out of the house and into the garage. I thought I heard the sound of mice. That put some fear in me, but I went in anyway. I'd placed Jiro's bicycle near the door, but it wasn't there. I didn't move for a second. I tried to feel around in the dark for the bicycle. I pushed something over and stood without moving as it—whatever it was—crashed on the floor. I could have just turned on the light, but my plan had been to keep the light off. Still, Jiro was almost sure to be asleep. I flicked on the light, spotted the bike, and flicked off the light. I didn't move for another moment. Then I felt my way over to where the bike was. I brought it out to the road and I set off. I had my roll of money with me and one change of clothes. If all went well, I'd be back before I'd need more.

I had never been out in nature that late by myself. It felt completely different from the only camping trip I'd ever taken, one time when Larry drove us all out to Colorado. That would have been fun, except I twisted my ankle on some rocks and fell into Marilyn, who fell down and sprained her wrist. So we had to go home instead of to Larry's cabin as we'd planned.

Right now all the trees surrounding me were kind of shocking and kind of cool at the same time. I was alone but also surrounded by bugs and animals and plants. Here and there a small house or business was illuminated with a dim light, but mostly, I used the moon or a flashlight to see the road. I pedaled frantically at first, then lazily as the breeze hit my face and hypnotized me. Then I noticed too late that a log lay on the road. I went flying over the bicycle handlebar and thudded to the ground. Fortunately, I landed on the soft dirt on the side of the road. Still, the noise from my fall echoed against the humid air.

Falling shook me up, shook up not just my body, but my head. It shook the fervor out of me and made me wonder what I was doing and why. And it made me scared. I closed my eyes and saw myself falling off the bicycle again. I opened my eyes. I'd gone this far, and I'd already told Maddie I was coming. So I knew I couldn't stop. I righted the bicycle and continued down the road.

Every so often I would catch glimpses of a river and see spots along the bed that seemed to be glowing. I figured it was just the moon shining off a wet spot, but still it was eerie.

I began sweating. I had to keep drying my palms on my clothes so I could grip the handles. Not a single vehicle passed in either direction.

When I reached the emporium, I laid my bike down behind the building. I wished I'd thought to bring a note to leave for Mrs. Sherwood, to let her know whose bicycle this was. But I figured that would all get sorted out eventually.

I squinted at my watch, saw the lone tiny diamond catch a light and sparkle. The time was one forty-five a.m.

The medical clinic down the road was actually open. At one point as I sat in the darkness, a car screeched up to the clinic. A doctor ran out while three men jumped from the car, one of them being supported by the other two. "He was trying to shoot a snake and accidentally shot his foot!" one of the men yelled. They all rushed inside.

I was not the least bit sleepy. I looked around. Everything around me seemed lush and wild, except for a potted plant bent in half over a rotted middle. Way down the road I saw a church cross outlined against the sky.

I shivered. I started to feel scared that some sheriffs would come to get me. Then I felt scared that they wouldn't come. I heard a bell and saw the clinic door opening. I jumped up and rushed around to the side of the store, trying to be as quiet as possible as I pressed hard against the wall. I felt like a secret agent.

I heard footsteps in the gravel. Unfortunately, the footsteps were getting closer. I would have run around to the back, but I didn't want to make any more noise. A man in a white smock shined a light on me. He came and stood right in front of me without saying a word at first. I just about wet my pants.

Finally, he spoke. "Nice night, isn't it?" His voice was a soothing drawl.

"Yes," I said.

He shook his head. "Man shot himself in the foot. It's not the dumbest thing I've ever seen, but it's pretty darn dumb." He stopped to think before continuing. "I guess the dumbest thing I've seen is the time Johnson got a bone the size of a golf ball stuck in his throat. Only the Lord knows how that happened and why he didn't choke to death."

I didn't reply, so the man continued.

"That was a Tuesday night he tried to swallow that bone. I'm only open one night and two days a week. I swear, some people just pick Tuesday nights to pull off their craziest stunts."

I still didn't reply.

"I'm Dr. Reed. Your father called me," he said. "He wants me to have you wait at the clinic."

One second I was thinking, *Rats, they caught me!* And the next second I was thinking, *Good, I was afraid nobody would catch me!* I heard rumbling down the way, and I knew it was the bus. In a minute it rumbled to a stop in front of the emporium. I saw a couple of sleepy faces in the windows. The driver opened the door. I imagined jumping aboard and shouting, *Let's go!* Instead, I stood sheepishly next to the doctor. I'd never run away before, so I didn't know how to act.

"Anybody getting on?" asked the driver.

"No, sir," said the doctor. The door closed and the bus rumbled on.

"Come along, young lady. Your father's on his way."

"My bike's around back."

"All right, I'm going to trust you because there's nowhere else to go. There's a bus that comes through at four a.m. bound for St. Louis, but I got a feeling you don't know anybody in St. Louis. Go get your bike and come over to the clinic."

I walked around back to pick up the bike, then walked with the doctor to the clinic, where I sat in a plastic seat not unlike the seats in the bowling alley near Larry's home. "Now I'm going to go in back," the doctor said. He left me alone. I didn't run away because he was right—I didn't know anybody in St. Louis.

"I wasn't trying to run away," I called out. "I was going to catch the bus and take care of some business downstate and then come back."

He didn't answer.

Someone drove up honking, and I assumed it was Jiro. But a young woman got out. The doctor entered the waiting area. "Grand Central Station here tonight," he said. He waited while the woman came in and showed him some marks on her chest.

"I fell on some umbrellas," she said.

"Mmm-hmm," he said, with neither doubt nor

belief. He looked at me and smiled slightly, then went in back with the woman while saying, "I haven't seen this much activity since I was in Vietnam."

I wondered what kind of punishment running away would deserve in Jiro's eyes. I took a big breath and thought about what I should say to him. But I couldn't think of anything. Then I thought I would just explain how Maddie's letters made me think I should go get her, but he wouldn't understand because he didn't really know Maddie. And I thought about how I needed to figure out what to do about her. Now I was back to thinking, *Rats!* But when Jiro's big old car pulled up, I stood up with the bicycle and followed my father, neither of us saying a word. I guess people talked less in Arkansas than in Chicago. But I knew he would have something to say.

The bicycle stuck out of the back trunk, but Jiro managed to fit it in there well enough that it wouldn't fall out. I opened up the passenger door and sat down, wondering what Jiro would do to punish me. He'd probably never punished someone before.

Jiro got in and started the drive back to his house. I stared out the window.

"Something's glowing out there by the river," I said, finally breaking a long silence between us.

"Earthworm mucus," he said gruffly.

"Oh!" He was angry. I said, "The clinic was busy. A man shot himself in the foot. He was trying to shoot a snake. And a woman fell on some umbrellas and had little round marks all over her chest."

"I never ask for you to be here," he said sharply. "I didn't want any more than you did."

I was surprised how much that stung. "I wasn't running away from you. It's just that, I mean, I'm responsible for Maddie. My mother told me so when Maddie was born. Marilyn takes care of Lakey, and I take care of Maddie. It's always been that way." I bit back tears. "She's my favorite sister, and I promised her I would come."

"Too young to make promise like that."

"I had no choice," I said, but he didn't reply.

He pulled up to his tiny house and we walked inside.

"Good night," I said when we reached the hallway to the bedrooms. "I wasn't trying to cause trouble."

"Good night." He said this last with fatigue, but also gently.

Before I went to sleep, I sat at the window and watched the trees sway in the wind and the goat sleep, and I thought I saw a small glowing patch way down below near the river. I couldn't imagine why earthworms would need to secrete glowing mucus. Could earthworms even see?

I got in bed. I wondered if Maddie was lying awake. Today she was a great sleeper, but as a baby she'd been a problem sleeper. That's how I'd come to take care of her so much. My mother needed to get her sleep, and I filled the void. Mom and I were like double-mothers of Maddie. I remembered staying up for hours with her to stop her crying and try to put her to sleep. I would carry her until my strength gave out, and sometimes I slept on the floor beside her crib, in case she needed me.

Had it only been a year ago that I'd been rushing across the country with my sisters on the way to Larry's? Now I was nearly fourteen. Last year I'd only been worried about Mr. Bronson's custody lawsuit. Now Maddie was living with him. How could things change so much in just one year? How could the whole world go from right side up to upside down?

I would have to think of something new. Maddie was going to be really upset when I didn't show up like I said I would. I could feel the wrinkles forming between my eyebrows. My mother said that area was one of the first to go. That's because people frowned too much. But who wouldn't frown? It was up to me to get Maddie away from Mr. Bronson. I wanted her to write me a real letter, not a letter written with her father lurking behind her. I wanted her to laugh and play and drive me crazy. That was my Maddie—not Mr. Bronson's Madeline.

I had a mysterious feeling that all four of us sisters were awake at that moment. "Hi, Maddie," I said out loud. "Hang in there. We'll figure something out. I promise."

chapter thirteen

I KNEW MADDIE WOULD HAVE waited for me for hours. Jiro left late for work, but the second he did, I pounced on the phone. Mr. Bronson answered. When I asked to speak to my sister, I heard him say, "It's Shelby." Then I heard her say, "I don't want to talk to her." He said to me, "She doesn't want to talk to you, Shelby."

"Can I please talk to her?"

"Shelby, she doesn't want to talk to you. I can't force her."

"Okay," I said. "Well, tell her to call me." I hung up. Darn it! If I could just explain to her what had happened, she wouldn't be mad at me anymore.

I called Maddie three times a day for the next

week, and nobody ever picked up. It was as if Mr. and Mrs. Bronson knew it was me on the line.

The next chain letter I got was started by Maddie, then went to Marilyn, then to me. But she'd written *Dear Marilyn and Lakey* in big letters across the top. My name wasn't there. She must have been really, really mad. Marilyn sent me the letter anyway. So I went outside to sit with my goat. I brought out paper and a pencil to write my portion of the letter. The goat pushed under my hand. I was *not* giving him my paper. But then I realized he wanted to be petted. He was awfully cute. Jiro said he was a pygmy goat. I petted him by massaging his head. He'd never let me pet him before. Every time I stopped, he would push under my hand again. Then in the middle of me petting him, he grabbed my paper and ran off.

I wondered whether I could find someplace near Chicago to stable him. I thought about how excited Maddie would be if, when we all came home, I had the goat with me! She wouldn't stay angry then. Jiro said some goats were domesticated but that it was really hard to house-train them. In a few minutes the goat returned without the paper. He lay down on top of one of my feet.

Then I started to wonder whether the Bronsons

read all of Maddie's incoming mail. I bet they did. That made it hard to write to her. I finally came up with this:

Dear Marilyn, Lakey, and Maddie,

You Know Who, don't be mad at me. I can explain everything.

Anyway, right now my goat is sitting on my foot. He really likes me. I like him too, although he's very demanding. Also, he ate Jiro's straw broom. Now it's just a stick. Jiro and I bought some goat food, and every day I feed some to my goat. I'm going to name him Goat.

Love,
Shelby

That's all I could think of to write without getting Maddie in trouble. This way she could deny that she was the one who was mad at me.

Then the next time I called her, Mr. Bronson picked up.

"Shelby, I was just thinking about you."

"Oh," was all I could think to say.

"Madeline's at her piano class."

"But she doesn't like piano class. She hated it when our mother made us take piano."

"That's news to me," Mr. Bronson replied. "Before I go, let me just say that I have a level of expertise on running away. I did it twice myself before I realized it's more trouble than it's worth."

"Okay, well. Bye."

"Good-bye," he said cheerfully.

Then that night I got a call from Mr. Bronson. He said a neighbor had seen Maddie climbing out a window and had run to stop her. She admitted she was running away and planned to live in Jiro's garage. He wanted to know whether I knew why Maddie was running away or whether she'd said anything to me about it. I said no, and later Marilyn called me and said Mr. Bronson had called her as well. I wrote to Maddie right away:

Dear Maddie,

It's dangerous for you to run away. You're really lucky that neighbor caught you. Mom is getting better, and pretty soon we'll all be back in Chicago. Just wait and see—it won't be long!

She didn't write me back, and Mr. Bronson repeatedly told me she was at a piano class, French class, crafts class, or tumbling class. Every day I checked for a return letter from her, but it never came.

For some reason the only thing that made me feel better was my goat. Sometimes he plopped down in my lap, licking my toes, his butt facing me. And whenever I wore a hat, he would take it from me. He'd just grab the hat and run off. I guess that was a goat's idea of humor. One day while I was out back talking to Goat, Jiro came home from work early. It wasn't even lunchtime yet. He usually got home from work around six. He looked at me, his jaw slack.

"Your mother sick," he said. "Have staph infection. We need to fly to Chicago."

"She has a what? What's that? I thought she was getting better. Who did you talk to?"

"Mack call me at work."

"Are you sure you heard right?"

"Yes, sure, yes. I ask him three times. Blood infected. Shelby, your mother . . . your mother might die from infection. We have to go."

"Die? You mean die like she'll be dead?"

He didn't answer as he seemed to be trying to

understand what I said. "Yes," he replied after a moment.

We just stood there looking at each other. I couldn't believe he'd heard right, so I rushed inside to call Marilyn. Nobody answered her phone. I called Larry, but his wife answered. It felt kind of weird to talk to her, but I had no choice. "Ashley, my dad says my mom has a staph infection. Is Larry there?"

"No, Larry just left with Lakey for the airport," Ashley said.

"Jiro says . . . Jiro says that my mother may die, but . . . well . . . Is that what Larry told you?"

"Well . . . Larry said that they can't seem to contain the infection. I'm so sorry."

"Well, okay, I'm sorry to bother you." I put the phone down, stunned.

It seemed I'd now been thrown into the parallel universe where people could die. I rushed outside to hug my goat. That made me feel a little better. Jiro ran out after me. "We need to leave. You pack now."

"Don't worry, I'll be back," I said to Goat. I turned to Jiro. "I'm going to leave him extra food. What exactly is a staph infection, anyway?"

"No, Goat will eat all food at once if you give. Staph infection is bacteriological, uh, I not really understand it myself. Never been in hospital. But your mother have it bad."

"Are my sisters all going to Chicago? I have to leave the goat something because he's used to getting food now."

"Yes, your sisters will be there. No can give goat extra food," he said firmly.

Ever since my mother's accident, it seemed like events were happening faster than I could catch up with them. I threw a few jeans and tank tops into my backpack, and I was ready to go. Jiro called out, "We need to leave now. Plane from Oklahoma."

As Jiro sped to the airport, it all caught up with me. My mother might die. I finally started crying. Jiro looked at me. "What happened?" he said.

"My mother might die! We have to hurry."

"We make flight on time, don't worry."

The more I tried to stop crying, the harder I cried. Tears seemed to leak out of my nose. Even my neck grew wet with tears. My mother always said my sisters cried with their eyes and I cried with my nose. My mother. Could. Die. I blew tears and snot out of my nose and onto my face. I didn't even know where you went when you died. We hadn't faced much death in our lives. Where would my mother go?

Would she try to talk to us? Half of what my head was filled with came from my mother. She taught us new things every day, like how to keep wrinkles from forming at the corners of our mouths, how to let a boy know you were interested without speaking, and how to smile without squishing your eyes. Even someone who thought she was a bad mother had to admit that my sisters and I were coming out fine. That was my mother's doing. Nobody could deny that we were proof that my mother was a good mother. And even if she wasn't a good mother, which she was, she'd created us since the moment we were born. As everything caught up with me, it was like I was suddenly in a tornado. And all the whirling air around me was my mother. Then I reached a moment of silence when I was in the middle of the tornado. I stopped crying and felt perfectly calm. Then I reached the other side of the tornado and started crying again.

"Good to cry," Jiro said, but I hardly heard him.

Then another horrible thought struck me. My sisters were in that tornado with me! If my mother died, I would lose them as well. We'd all have to stay with our fathers! Then I thought of how vulnerable my mother was. I'd never thought that before. But really, beneath her confidence, she was just as delicate as anyone else. I didn't care what anybody said, I didn't care what Bronson's custody papers said. My mother was a good mother because we had all been happy together. I started wailing.

"Don't lose mind," Jiro said suddenly. "Cry but don't lose mind."

I felt like I *could* lose my mind. Then the tornado passed, and I was exhausted. It was like every ounce of liquid had come out of me. I couldn't breathe through my nose at all. I felt older somehow, but I didn't know how. I didn't know what had changed in me that made me feel older. Maybe I would know later.

Jiro was talking. I heard him saying, "Healthy as a horse. She won't die."

"Do you promise?" I demanded.

"Yes. I promise."

And I believed that somehow he knew my mother couldn't die. That calmed me a bit, but my gut still ached. I felt the worst for Maddie. I couldn't even imagine what kind of turmoil she'd been going through and was going through now. That thought made me feel older because I could see Maddie emerging from all this older, more formed. I ached so much for my Maddie that I started crying all over again. I didn't want to lose her to Mr. Bronson.

I started to think that my mother could die after all. And I thought I had to remember every little thing going on now, because later I would want to know how it all felt. Every precious moment when she was alive was better than a million moments when she was dead. Who wanted a long life if you were sad? I had a lot of deep thoughts, if I say so myself.

The car followed the curving highway through the Ozarks. The hills were intensely green, and occasionally, we'd see a lake beneath us.

Jiro said, "Some people call Ozarks mountains, but Ozarks are plateau that was carved by water. So we not driving through mountains, but over valleys."

I set that aside in my brain as one of the details I might want to remember someday. And suddenly I wanted to know how Jiro met my mother; I wanted to know more about my mother.

"Do you still like my mom?" I asked him.

I could see his eyes go wide for a moment. Then it took him another moment to say, "I never know her well. Many people never know her well."

I chewed on that without saying more. "I don't even know how you two met."

"In Las Vegas airport, Japanese sightseeing tour. We all see your mother at same time and staring at her. She pick me out for some reason."

"So I was, you know, uh . . ."

"You conceived in Las Vegas. We got married, then got annulment. Then we both go home."

I just gazed out the window; I didn't know how to respond.

I loved being engulfed in the Ozarks, with no people or cars before or behind us. I felt like I was in a circle of peace. And then the Ozarks ended and we weren't alone anymore, weren't at peace. As we left the Ozarks, we were back in civilization and I was going to Chicago in case my mother died.

My mother was a strong woman. I had never seen her express fear. And that was what she would want from me too. I had to be strong for myself and for my younger sisters. Maybe that was part of how I'd changed. I felt more responsibility now. It was up to me to win Maddie back and make her happy again. Mr. Bronson was slapping her down, and I had to make sure she wasn't permanently harmed. That's what I had to do. That's what my mom would do.

"What thinking?" Jiro said.

"I don't know for sure," I said. I had the most trivial

thought. I thought I wanted to know why he dressed the way he did, but asking would seem rude, so I didn't ask.

Later I stared out the plane window. I was all mixed up. Right there on the plane everything felt calm and normal. But the second I left this plane, I would be back in the real world. I started sobbing again. Jiro didn't speak, just let me sob and sob. I blurted out to a stewardess, "My mother was in a car accident!" The stewardess said she was sorry and, as if it would make me feel better, brought me some more peanuts.

Walking down the ramp after our arrival, Jiro said, "Never meet Lakey or Marilyn father."

Mack and Marilyn met us at the gate. I thought I'd be excited to see Marilyn, and I was excited, but more than that, I was relieved. All that time I was yearning to be with my sisters, and now, finally, it was going to happen, but it was all because our mother might die. I ran toward Marilyn and we hugged and laid our foreheads on each other's. Mack said, "What is this? Some kind of mind meld?"

"Are you okay? You look terrible," Marilyn said. "Don't worry. Mom's a strong person."

Her eyes were also red, but Marilyn was so beautiful that even when she cried, she looked good.

"When are Maddie and Lakey coming?" I said.

"We're going to go meet Lakey's plane now. Maddie's lands in another hour."

Mack shook Jiro's hand. "I admire the Japanese," Mack said, apropos of nothing. Jiro nodded, looking a little confused.

I turned to Marilyn. "What happened to Mom? On Tuesday you said she was okay."

"I don't know. She *was* okay. She was complaining about not being able to wear any makeup during surgery. And then the doctor called this morning and said for us to come as soon as possible."

"Can she really die?" I said, a tremor in my voice.

"That's what Dr. Jefferson said. They've been removing dead tissue every few days or so, and there was one area that just wasn't healing. So they did yet another skin graft, but the skin died and the open wound got infected."

Wow, that sounded horrible: an open, infected wound. That's not how I imagined her injury at all. Kevin Kelly, a boy in my class, broke his arm one time and he never had an open wound. I knew because we sat next to each other at school and he told me what it was like to have a broken arm. But my mother didn't do anything like other people. She didn't even have a broken arm like a normal person.

"Is it the doctor's fault? Should we take her to a different hospital?"

"No, it's nobody's fault," Marilyn said.

We went to Lakey's gate, and when she arrived, we did a group hug, leaning on one another so that if one of us moved, we'd all fall over. We walked arm in arm to Maddie's gate, speaking our secret language so our fathers wouldn't know what we were saying.

"Iihthegis Mihthegistuhthegir Bruhthegonsthegon stuhthegill spuhthegankthegíng Muhthegadduhthegie?" Lakey asked. It took me a second to get that one: Is Mr. Bronson still spanking Maddie?

"Uh-huh," I said. "You don't have to call him 'mthegisttheger.'" I didn't tell her that I always called him "mister." I lowered my voice even more, and we slowed down until the fathers were several feet in front of us. "He isn't like our fathers at all." My eyes got teary again. "Maddie will be . . . she'll be the worst off if Mom . . . if she . . . if it's not okay . . ."

Marilyn's face grew grim. "Her letters are getting so weird, don't you think?"

"I think Mr. Bronson is dictating them," I said.

Our fathers stopped walking until we caught up, and we all clustered at Maddie's gate. Mack muttered to himself with an unlit cigarette hanging off his lips.

Jiro was chewing a piece of gum thoughtfully, as if he might be testing it. Larry drank from a can of soda.

As we waited I put my weight on one foot and then the other, one and then the other, swaying back and forth nervously. It'd been two entire weeks since Maddie had last spoken to me. What if she still wouldn't, now?

Finally, Maddie's plane arrived. We spied Mr. Bronson first, then Maddie walking a few steps behind him. He looked even larger than I remembered. Jiro, Mack, and Larry shook hands with him.

"Hi, Maddie," I said, hurrying over to her.

"Hi," she said coolly.

I could feel Mr. Bronson's eyes on us.

"How are you?" I said.

"I'm fine, thank you."

I bit my lip, trying not to cry, and leaned over to try to hug her. She just stood there as I wrapped my arms around her.

"Maddie. Are you okay?"

"Yes."

I said much more softly, "Are you mad at me?" She nodded her head yes.

Mack said, "I'll take Larry and Lakey along with Marilyn, and the rest of you can take a taxi."

"No!" Marilyn, Lakey, and I cried. Marilyn pulled at her father's arm, "We want to ride together."

"Let them ride together," Mr. Bronson said authoritatively.

So Mack took us girls and the other three fathers took a taxi. Mack drove like the entire world was in a conspiracy against him. As soon as he got onto the road, he cried out, "What?! First he turns on his left signal and then he goes right! Why did he do that to me?" Then, when somebody turned on their signal and tried to get in front of Mack, he accelerated and said, "Oh, no you don't."

My sisters and I were eerily quiet on the drive from the airport. I'd never been with my sisters when we were so quiet. And it was weird, but they looked slightly different than I remembered them. Marilyn changed from parting her hair in the middle to the side. Maddie's hair was longer and matted down. Lakey's hair was shorter and her face seemed thinner. I guess the month we'd been separated changed us all. I could have made small talk, but that would have seemed even weirder than our silence. We must have been changing a little bit every day, and all the little changes added up so that now we were different. It was as if I didn't know them 100 percent anymore. I knew them only 95 percent now.

We'd already missed afternoon visiting hours at the ICU, and evening visiting hours didn't start again until eight p.m., so we were going to the apartment to drop off our bags first. When we got there, the other fathers had already arrived. Mack said to Marilyn, "See? They got here first because we ran into all the worst drivers on the road."

The apartment I'd grown up in felt odd to me too. It looked different, just like my sisters did. It felt kind of like the ghost town that one of my mother's boyfriends took us to once. We girls threw our bags into our bedroom and then went into the living room to see—well, we weren't sure what we would see.

In the living room Mack was scribbling something on a notepad. "He's writing his feelings down," Marilyn whispered to me. "It's for his shrink."

The other fathers were standing quietly. Over time our fathers had grown more what they were. In other words, Mr. Bronson had grown more stiff, my father had grown both more Japanese and more Southern, Mack more emotional, and Larry more wonderful, handsomer, stronger. For the first time ever, all the dads stood together in our living room. They didn't do much except politely offer one another the best seat—the fake-leather recliner—and then even more politely offer one another the bowl of cashews that Marilyn had scrounged out of the cupboard. There was the couch, which was where we girls sat, three chairs we'd brought in from the dining room, and the recliner.

Mr. Bronson lowered himself majestically into the recliner as if it were his throne. He talked about the future and the way of the world while we girls dutifully listened. "I've raised three children and consider myself an expert in child-rearing. And I can tell you that a dose of reality is all a part of growing up." As he went on and on, I noticed that Maddie wouldn't look at her father's face. The gist of Mr. Bronson's talk seemed to be that we girls were about to visit our mom, and this would help us learn the way of the world. I felt a twisting in my gut. I wondered whether Mr. Bronson was right the way he always thought he was. I didn't know for sure what the way of the world was. Maddie and I looked at each other, but she didn't change her grim expression. The area between her eyebrows was all squished up with worry. Then she turned away, still grim.

"Now that we're all together," Mack said. "I can tell you all what's going on. When we get to the hospital, they're going to let us see Helen two at a time. They've tried a variety of antibiotics on the infection, but they haven't found one that will kill the staph." His voice broke and his eyes grew wet. "I'm usually very manly," he said. "Anyway, it's a drug-resistant kind of infection, and it seems to have spread from her arm to her blood. We should get going." It was after seven by now. Mack continued, "I'll drive the girls over, and you gentlemen can grab a taxi to Cook County Memorial Hospital."

"All right," said Larry. "Let's go, then."

We hurried after Mack to his car.

"Before this morning I had never even heard of a staph infection," I said.

"Me neither," Marilyn said.

"I'm feeling worried about your mother," Mack said. "I have to write more about that later. The doctor thinks I might still be in love with her without owning it." None of us spoke. "Hello? Am I talking to myself?"

"Dad, of course we're all listening," Marilyn said. She turned around from the passenger seat, looked at us girls in back. "Is everyone okay?"

"Yeah," Lakey and I said.

Maddie just looked out the window, her face pale and sad. I didn't know how far away she was, or how far I would need to pull her back before she was ours again.

chapter fourteen

AT THE HOSPITAL WE FOLLOWED Mack to the waiting room outside of intensive care. While he talked to the nurse, the other fathers showed up looking grim. I didn't know if they were grim because of my mother's condition or because of something that had been said in the taxi.

Mack turned to us girls and said, "Okay, which two of you want to see her first? How about Shelby and Maddie?"

Mr. Bronson said, "I'll make all decisions regarding Madeline." He paused. "All right, you may go, Madeline."

Mack walked up to the nurse with us and said, "These two are going first. She's their mother."

The nurse walked us down a short corridor and into a brightly lit room where our mother lay in the center on a narrow bed. I ran to the bed, but the nurse reprimanded me. "Be gentle."

It took a lot of self-control not to gasp when I saw my mom. She was attached to an IV; she'd lost a lot of weight; her cheeks and forehead and free hand were covered with a rash and open sores; stitches lined the left side of her face; and her right arm hung in traction, the cast covered by a white sock, with only three fingertips peeking out. For a moment I just gaped at her. She seemed like someone who resembled our mother but wasn't really her.

Our mother smiled sleepily at us. "Oh, I've missed you girls. Maddie, my baby. And Shelby. Don't worry, I'll be fine. I can't wait to get out of here. I miss you girls!"

Maddie stood back as if she didn't know how she'd gotten here and wasn't sure where she was. A nurse came in with rubber gloves and gave me a pair. I put them on and held my mother's left hand. I tried not to stare at her face. But I didn't do a very good job because Mom said, "It's the infection. It caused a rash. Shelby, look at you. In one month you've changed. More grown up." She shook her head and blinked back tears.

She looked so thin and wan that I couldn't think of anything positive to say. All I could come up with was, "Mom, you look, I mean I hope, well, I know you'll get better."

"They're pumping me with antibiotics." She paused. "But if I don't . . ."

"But you will," I said. "Jiro says you're healthy as a horse."

"He said I look like a 'horse'?"

"No, Mom. He meant you were really healthy."

"But he said 'horse'?"

"Mom, never mind. He didn't say anything."

"You girls need to listen for a minute. If worse comes to worst, I want you girls to know that whatever anyone says, I've done my best with you. And I couldn't be prouder of you."

"Mom, stop it," I said.

"But the most important thing I want to say is that I know in my heart that your fathers will take care of you. Jiro is a dear man, and Harvey Bronson, while not dear, is a responsible, respected man."

"Mom, we all have to be together again. We were happy that way."

"It was fun, wasn't it?" my mother said. Her eyelids fluttered—sleepily.

I was at a loss for words. Then I decided that if she was going to die, this was my last chance to save Maddie. "Mom, couldn't you just let Maddie and me live with Jiro? Couldn't you just tell that to Mr. Bronson? He's here, you could tell him now. You won't have to fight him. You could just tell him."

"Shelby, you have no idea how much trouble that man can cause. I *will* get better, and then after you girls are back with me, I'll give him a piece of my mind."

"But he's destroying Maddie," I said.

"Of course he's not destroying her."

Tears dribbled down Maddie's face, but still she didn't say a word.

"I miss you girls more than you can imagine. Don't make me worry, Shelby. I wanted to see you girls to make me feel at peace, not to worry me."

I had temporarily run out of steam. "Yes," was all I could say.

She said, "We had a lot of fun, didn't we?"

"Mom, when you get better, which you will, we'll still have fun. You just have to go to a parallel universe. You were in the universe where beauty was the most important thing, and now you can go to the universe where it isn't."

"Ain't no such universe," my mother said. "God, I'm tired."

"There is so. I'm in that universe! You'll still be beautiful, just not perfect. Shouldn't you be in the same universe we're all in? Then we can all be together."

She started crying. "I had so much fun."

The nurse came in. "Are you upsetting her?"

"No!" I exclaimed.

"I think we better send your sisters in," the nurse said anyway.

Rats, rats, rats. I left as my mother was wiping away tears. I had said everything wrong and made her cry. I was an idiot.

But the nurse put her arm around me and said, "Time to go, sweetie."

I squeezed my mother's hand. "I didn't want to upset you," I said.

"I'll be fine, and then everything will be back to normal." That wasn't like my mother at all. Usually she came up with a good cliché, like "Keep a stiff upper lip."

Next Marilyn and Lakey went inside. Mack had

his usual unlit cigarette between his lips as he paced back and forth in the waiting area. Larry and Jiro were talking about the beautiful oaks that were getting cut down in Arkansas. Mr. Bronson sat with his arms crossed on his chest. He looked angry, but then, he always looked angry. Maddie separated herself from us and stood alone a few feet from the chairs. She rocked back and forth, her face a total blank. I knew that if my mother died, we would never win Maddie back.

Finally, Mr. Bronson snapped, "I never heard of taking a child your age to see someone in intensive care."

"I'm sorry, sir," Maddie said meekly.

I wanted to shout at her, *You don't have to call him "sir"!* Instead, I just looked at Maddie.

"Did you make your mother cry?" Mr. Bronson said crisply to me.

"We had a private conversation."

"Here's the thing, Shelby. You are the least psychologically developed adolescent I've ever met."

My father sighed, as if he might now be drawn into the argument. "My daughter good girl," he said. "Very advanced."

"She needs some discipline," Mr. Bronson said.

"She my daughter, I raise her my way."

"I could help you with that. Maddie is my fourth."

"No need help," Jiro said curtly, so curtly that he even managed to shut up Mr. Bronson.

A few moments later, the nurse came back with Marilyn and Lakey. "When can we visit Helen?" Larry asked her.

"I think she's a little too agitated now for more visitors," the nurse said. "Hopefully tomorrow. I'm sorry, but she needs to rest."

"Oh, I can't stand this," Marilyn cried. "I need to get some air." Maddie, Lakey, and I hurried after her down the hall. Once outside, I looked up at the moon and tried to let that beautiful glow inside my heart, but it wouldn't fit. I noticed a couple of other people gazing up at the sky to see what I was looking at. And then I looked at my hands, at my feet, and at the moon again. It was hard to believe I was real. It was hard to believe any of this could be real. I wonder if my mother felt the same way.

At home Marilyn didn't call one of our powwows. When I asked her to, she said no. It was the strangest thing. For a month all we'd wanted was to get back together, and now that we were, we didn't know what to do. We didn't know how to be together anymore. Or maybe what we needed to talk about was too big to talk about.

Maddie picked up her pajamas and said, "I'll change in the facilities." She walked out of the room.

"The 'facilities'?" I echoed.

"I think she means the bathroom," said Lakey.

"I *know* that. I mean, who goes to the facilities to put on their jammies?" I said.

"She's acting really weird," Lakey whispered.

"We have to get her away from Bronson somehow," I said.

"Shhh," Marilyn hissed.

We heard a door close, and Maddie walked in wearing her pajamas, the pair with the pink feet that made her look like an imp. She wore those jammies all the time, even when it was summer. For a second I thought she was back to normal.

I took her hands and led her to her bed. "Maddie," I said, "the day I didn't show up to get you, I *did* try to run away, but I got caught. Jiro was *so* mad at me! But I really did try. I went out in the middle of the night to the bus stop. I really, really tried."

"Okay," Maddie said.

"Are you mad at me?"

"No." Then she said in a monotone, "Good night,

everybody. Pleasant dreams." Now that was what she always said, except not in a monotone. Usually when she said good night, she said it in such a chipper voice that I thought she was wide awake. But as soon as she hit the pillow, she was always out.

But as we lay in our beds quietly, I could feel Maddie awake while Marilyn and Lakey slept. "Maddie?" I said.

"What?"

"Are you okay?"

"What do you mean?"

"I mean, are you okay?"

"I don't know what you mean," she said.

So I closed my eyes and saw my mother in the hospital. It was almost as if I could even see things I hadn't noticed when I was actually there. Like I could see not only how awful Mom looked, but also how far away Maddie stood from me and how her face was a total blank. Now I heard Maddie's breathing settle, and I knew I was the last one awake.

Next morning the first thing I heard was pounding on our door. My heart stopped for a moment. Pounding on a door was always a bad thing.

"What?" Marilyn called out.

"Are you all decent?" It was Mack.

"Yeah, Dad."

The door opened, and Mack stood there looking cheerful. "Good news, the new antibiotic is working. Your mother seems to be rallying. Her fever broke last night. I just got the news from Dr. Jefferson. Ah, the world is a fair place sometimes. I'm going to write about that tonight."

We all jumped up. "Is it for sure?" I asked excitedly.

"For sure and then some. The doctor is surprised how she's surging back. She's going to make it, girls."

Relief flooded me. It was like yesterday the world was a bad place and today it was a good place. I actually understood Mack for the first time. The world was a fair place sometimes.

"Yep, she's over the hump," Mack continued. "Hey, that would make a good song title. 'Over the Hump.'" Marilyn and I had to laugh at that one, and he looked offended. "I thought about being a songwriter before I bought my restaurant."

"Dad, that's a great song title." Marilyn looked at me and smiled, and I smiled back.

Mack looked at me. "Now, Shelby, don't be making your mother cry when you visit her today."

"I won't. I promise. Well, I don't promise, but I'll try really hard."

"Okay, get dressed so we can get there before noon." I looked at the clock in our room. It was ten a.m. And then I looked around again in alarm.

"Where's Maddie?" I asked Mack.

"She's been up since five studying with her father. Poor kid. She looked flat-out exhausted when he woke her up."

And that's when I decided. I didn't know what to do, I didn't know how to do it, but I did know there was no way Maddie was going back to Arkansas with Mr. Bronson.

"We need to powwow about Maddie," I hissed to Marilyn the moment Mack left the room.

"Okay, later," she agreed.

Once dressed, we hurried into the kitchen to see what smelled so good. Mack was making French toast and singing. He sang like he did everything: with his whole self but not very well. Maddie was already at the kitchen table, her hands in her lap, waiting for breakfast. Mr. Bronson sat next to her, a napkin tucked into his collar.

"Oh, they finally get dressed," Mack teased. "The sleeping beauties finally make it out of bed."

Larry picked up
"I'm happy for you gi
you."

"So what else did the
Marilyn asked.

"Just the most important
"She's over the hump. You girls
your homes tonight. Bronson says
fine he needs to get back to teach his
Get back? But we'd just gotten here.

After breakfast we all headed to the
Mack was in great form, yelling with abandon
window at anyone he felt had offended him,
was quite a few people.

I have to say, I'd never understood what my mother saw in Mack, but now I found myself actually liking the man.

And despite his driving, we got to the hospital first. He took the steps two by two, then grasped a nurse's hand and kissed it, saying, "Thank you for taking such good care of my ex-girlfriend. I would marry you if I didn't love her."

The nurse couldn't help smiling. My sisters and I laughed.

Mack headed off toward my mother's room when a

d out, "We moved her out of intensive care. 02. But it's not quite visiting hours yet."

'll have to call security to keep us from visit- now."

e nurses didn't call security, and we all walked oom 402. I was surprised that our mother looked tly as she had the day before. But Mack couldn't subdued. He air-kissed her. "My ravishing ex, how ce to see you on this beautiful morning."

She smiled. Anyway, her teeth were still beautiful. She had the most perfect smile of anyone I'd ever seen. Maddie's smile was more wonderful, but not as perfect.

"I'm so relieved, Mom," Marilyn said, sinking into the chair beside her.

"Me too," I said, bouncing on the balls of my feet.

"I don't know what all the fuss was about," Mom said. "I was never planning to die."

"Of course you weren't," Mack boomed. "You'll outlive us all!"

"Mack, you're funny," she said, almost flirtatiously.

The others showed up just then. Mr. Bronson stopped at the door, looked at us, looked down at Maddie. "We're not supposed to be in here." He

leaned in the room to take Maddie's hand and said, "We'll wait outside until the nurse says it's okay."

He led Maddie out of the room.

Jiro walked in anyway. He looked down at my mom and said, "Happy for you. Too strong to die."

"Shelby told me you said I was strong like a horse."

He looked trapped for a second, then said, "You very strong. Always very strong." He laughed. "You beat me arm wrestling once!"

Mom wanted us to stay with her for a little while, so we all noisily tried to do a crossword puzzle together and got only three words. Even Jiro yelled excitedly when he got one of the words. "I read dictionary!" he said. "I read dictionary!" Mr. Bronson and Maddie came in when the nursed okayed it. They sat quietly, awkwardly, and as I watched Mr. Bronson sitting so straight and so stiff, I realized something: He was shy. But before I could think further about this, the nurses kicked us out for being too loud.

chapter fifteen

AT HOME THAT EVENING WE needed a serious powwow. Marilyn said, "She's on a high right now, but she may be brought down to earth when she really studies her scars."

"She could be in the parallel universe where beauty doesn't matter," I said.

"There's no universe like that!" Marilyn said.

"Yes, there is," I insisted. Then, just as I'd said to my mother, I told Marilyn, "I'm in that universe."

"No, you're not. We're all in the same universe. It's a small one—the only people in it are the four of us and Mom."

"I'm in the universe where beauty doesn't matter," I said stubbornly.

"Mom *is* her beauty," Marilyn said.

"No, she's not," I said.

Marilyn looked annoyed. "All right, let's move on. Let's get back to the main subject of this meeting, which is our dads."

Lakey said, "My turn! I love my dad, but I feel out of place at his house. His wife is polite to me and I have to be polite to her, but I can't really act like me. And it's not fun like it is with all of you. I have to behave phony."

Marilyn said, "My dad's okay, but he's kind of a nut."

We fell silent. I thought for a moment. What did I think about Jiro? I guess I felt he was embarrassing but that it wasn't his fault. He didn't actually have a lot of faults besides dressing badly and talking funny.

Maddie said, "I have to pee." She waited. "May I?" she said.

"Of course," we all said.

She got up and left the room.

"Who asks for permission before they pee?" I said.

"Bronson probably makes her," Marilyn said.

"But why anybody would ask? Wouldn't the answer always be yes? You can't say no if somebody has to pee."

"Maddie's acting weird," Lakey said for about the fourth time in two days.

"That's the real reason we're having this meeting," Marilyn said. "We need to find a time we can powwow without Maddie. Maybe we should meet after she falls asleep."

When Maddie walked back in, nobody spoke. She looked around at us suspiciously.

"Okay, meeting is adjourned," Marilyn said.

"Is that it? Did I miss anything?" Maddie said.

"Nope," we all said.

"Boy, I'm tired," I said. "How about you, Maddie?"

"I can go to sleep if you think I should."

"What do you mean?" I said. "It's really up to you if you're tired."

"I guess I'm tired."

"Okay," I said. "Then let's all go to sleep."

We all got in our pajamas, Maddie changing in the bathroom. Someone knocked at the door. "Come in," said Marilyn.

Larry entered and gave Lakey a kiss. Then he came over and gave each of us a kiss before saying, "If your mother is still doing well tomorrow, Mr. Bronson and Jiro need to get back, so Maddie and

Shelby will be leaving the day after tomorrow. You and I can stay a couple of days longer if you want."

"I want to stay as long as I can," Lakey said.

"That's what I thought. We'll do that. I don't need to get back for a few days." He kissed her again and left the room.

We all lay in bed. I could feel that Marilyn and Lakey were still awake. Finally, Marilyn said, "Maddie?"

She didn't answer, so Marilyn, Lakey, and I got up. Marilyn cracked the door and then said, "They're watching TV. We'll have to stay in here. Just talk quietly."

We sat near Marilyn's bed. "It's like she has two personalities," Lakey said.

Marilyn said, "It's like she's a Stepford daughter."

"A what?" Lakey said.

"It's like she's a robot."

"I think we need to get her out of there," I said. "We can't let her go back with Mr. Bronson."

"I agree," Marilyn said. "But what can we do?"

"We can all run away together," I said. Neither sister said no, I noticed.

Marilyn said, "Nothing feels right or normal with Mack. It kind of drives me crazy. And even if it didn't,

Maddie needs to be with us. It's like she's at a military school or something! I almost want to shake her and say 'Where's Maddie!'"

"I know! That's exactly how I feel." And so I asked, "Where could we go if we ran away?"

We all thought for a moment, and then Lakey said, "How about Larry's cabin in Colorado?"

"Do you know how to get there?" Marilyn asked. I leaned forward; I could detect a note of possibility in Marilyn's voice.

"I can find it without the address. I remember the street name. It was called Mountain View Road. The only thing is, one day I threatened to run away to the cabin. So Larry might know where we're going."

It wasn't a bad idea in my estimation, but it wasn't a good idea, either. Still, it was the only idea we had so far. "There's Jiro's garage," I suggested.

"We can't live in a garage," Marilyn said.

We all fell silent. I looked at my funny feet and wondered whether I'd inherited them from Jiro. I would feel bad running away because he'd been awfully nice to me. On the other hand, Maddie's welfare was the most important thing.

"Okay, I vote for Larry's cabin," I said. "It sounds perfect. Where else are we going to go? Maybe we could leave a note with the fathers saying we're fine and not to tell Mom because she'd get too upset."

Lakey said, "I agree. I don't want to live with Larry and his wife. I want to live with you." Then she started crying. Then Marilyn and I started crying.

Larry peeked into the room. "Everything all right in here?" he said. "Girls, girls, you don't need to worry about your mother. The doctor is very optimistic. I spoke to him on the phone just a little while ago." Then he looked right at Lakey. "Are you okay, sweetheart?"

"Yes," she said through her tears. "We were just talking."

"All right," he said. "Call if you need anything." He closed the door.

Lakey rubbed her eyes. "I miss you guys. It's so lonely out there. I can't stand it."

"How would we get to the cabin? Should we take a bus?" I said.

We looked at Marilyn. "I'll have to drive," she said. "I have a set of my dad's car keys. Maybe it's better to go right away when they don't expect it. Shelby, you need to tell Maddie when she wakes up tomorrow."

"Wait, what did we just decide?" I said.

"That we'll leave sometime after we visit Mom tomorrow."

The next day our mother was doing even better. When we arrived, she was ordering two nurses around. "No, no, make the head of the bed higher. The blood is going to my face and making it look bloated. Where's my water? I need to clean all the drugs out of my system. There's nothing more aging than drugs."

The nurses shook their heads with annoyance but did as she asked. They left, and we gathered around our mother.

"Dr. Jefferson is such a nice man," she said. "He brought me a flower today." She indicated a flower in a plastic cup. "He said he got it from his own house. I wonder where he lives. Of course, if we all moved in, I would need to put my own touches on the house, but I shouldn't say more because it's bad luck to put the cart before the horse." She smiled broadly, the most cheerful I'd seen her since the accident. I was so glad to see her smile. But I also knew that if Mom was getting better, truly, then we had to leave. Today.

Back at the apartment, Mr. Bronson announced that he'd booked a return flight back to Arkansas. "Madeline, it's a nine o'clock flight. Have your things packed before you go to bed. Now let's start your reading lesson." She followed him into the kitchen.

I rubbed my temples. Marilyn caught my eye. "Tonight," she mouthed. I nodded.

We three older girls powwowed in our room without Maddie. "Okay, let's take a final vote," Marilyn said. "If we are going to do this, if we are going to Colorado, it needs to be tonight. So, are we leaving? Yes or no?"

"I vote yes," I said.

"Me too," Lakey said.

"Me too," Marilyn said.

We returned to the living room, acting as normal as possible so the fathers wouldn't think we were plotting anything. All afternoon we watched soap operas and talk shows with Jiro and Larry. Jiro fell asleep three times and Larry fell asleep twice. At one point Jiro said, "No understand Americans. Why they go on talk shows and embarrass themselves?"

"I think they like to be on television," I said.

"Why they like that?"

"I don't know. I don't want to be on television."

"I do," said Marilyn. "After I'm famous, I'll go on television all the time."

"What will you be famous for?"

"I haven't decided yet."

Then we fell silent again, lying like sloths around the TV. It was hard to believe we would be running away that night. We were doing a darn good job of acting normal.

When Maddie finished her lessons, Larry went into the kitchen to cook us what he called his "special ultradelicious tacos."

The news shows were on, and we just kept watching TV. Mr. Bronson scolded us: "You girls should be doing something. You need some fresh air instead of lying around inside all day. Get out of the house and get some exercise!"

We just looked at him.

"But Larry's about to serve dinner," Marilyn said.

"After dinner, then. I don't want to see you lying around all night. It's repulsive."

After dinner all four of us went downstairs and sat on the stoop. Marilyn and I met eyes. "Maddie," I said, in a careful voice. "We have a plan."

"A plan?" she said. "A plan about what?"

"Well, a plan that's a big secret."

She looked at me suspiciously. "What kind of secret?"

"Can you promise you won't tell your father?"

"I can't promise," she said right away.

"Why?"

"Because he's my father, so he's the boss."

"Why?"

"Because he said . . . whatever, I don't know."

"Why?"

"Because I don't know him that well and I don't, I don't know, uh . . ."

"Why?"

"You're playing Why? with me!" Her eyes sparkled but then died out.

I said, "Ythegou uhthegalmthegost smthegiled."

Then she did smile, but only slightly. I smiled back.

Now she just looked curious, not suspicious. "Why can't I tell anyone?" she asked.

"Because it's a secret between the four of us."

She pondered that. "All right."

"You promise you won't tell on us?" I asked.

"Yes."

Marilyn said, "Good! Here's the plan. I'm going to drive Mack's car, and the four of us are going to go away together. We'll come back when Mom can take care of us again."

"We can't do that!" Maddie said. "I'll get in trouble. I have to tell my father!"

"You promised!" we all said.

"That's because you tricked me." She stood up.

I stood up too. "Maddie. You can't tell him. Please?"

She sat down again and didn't answer.

Marilyn leaned forward, her eyes gleaming. "We're going to Larry's cabin in Colorado." She sat back proudly.

Maddie looked interested. In fact, she looked very interested.

"It won't be for long. Just until Mom's better, and she's already getting better now."

"Like how long?" Maddie said.

"Like a month or so," I said.

"Yeah, a month," Marilyn said.

"And how would we get food?"

"With our money," I said.

Marilyn, Lakey, and I looked at Maddie. Her lips moved as she thought about it, and I could tell she was repeating it to herself as if she couldn't yet fully comprehend it all.

Finally, I said, "Maddie, are you in or out?"

Maddie said, "You mean we wouldn't tell our fathers?"

"That's right," I said. I sat in front of her and took both her hands in mine. "Maddie, sweetie, we're running away."

"I need to ask my father first."

"Maddie, running away means you don't tell your father anything."

"But he won't be happy with me."

"Maddie," I said. "Maddie, this is important and you can't tell Mr. Bronson."

"Why not?"

"Because he'll stop us and then . . ." I wanted to say *and then you'll never be the same.* She'd changed so much in a month, who knew what would happen in a couple more months? Our mother wouldn't be able to take care of us just because she was getting better. She still needed to have her plastic surgeries.

"We need to do it tonight," Marilyn said.

"We could leave at any time," I said. "Depending on when the fathers go to sleep. Jiro is always in bed by ten and up at five."

"Mack is in bed by midnight and up at six."

"My dad is usually in bed by eleven and up at six," Lakey said.

Maddie was frowning deeply. I repeated, "You can trust us."

"Mr. Bronson is in bed by ten and up at five," she finally said reluctantly.

"So we should leave around two in the morning," Marilyn said. "Let's go to bed right now so at least we can get some rest."

"I don't go to bed until eight thirty," Maddie said. "My father says it's a good idea to go to sleep at the exact same time every night, or you'll get off schedule."

Marilyn looked at her. "Okay, let's get in bed in our clothes, and you don't have to go to sleep. You can just lie there. We'll set the alarm for two in the morning." She turned to me. "Shelby, you're in charge of getting us there. Do you remember the highways?"

"No, and all the maps are in Mom's room!" I said. Mr. Bronson was sleeping in there.

"Okay, we'll buy a map on the road. And Lakey is in charge of hotels and money, and Maddie can watch the gas gauge. Just like always. Whenever we spend any money, you should write it down, Lakey. Did anyone bring their money?"

"I did," I said.

"Me too," Lakey and Marilyn said.

"I don't know where he put my money," Maddie said. "Anyway, I'm too young to handle money."

"Says who?" I asked.

"My father told me so," she said, a little defensively.

I was afraid she was going to snitch on us, but she

didn't move. It was kind of like we were kidnapping her, but it was for her own good.

Later I lay in bed thinking. I think thinking was my favorite thing in the world. At least, I think so. I hoped that a little bit of the real Maddie was still alive. Otherwise, she might turn us in. Another thing I thought about was my mother. I was certain that she was wrong and that there were some universes where beauty wasn't important. But if she didn't believe it, she would be depressed. She would cry more. Seeing your mother cry seemed all wrong. We girls could cry, but not our mother. She had always been strong, even tough, beneath her looks. Then the next thing I knew, I was dreaming about my goat when a voice came from the sky: "Shelby, get up. Shelby." I jolted awake. The light was on. Lakey was leaning over me, her face filled with urgency. "This is it," she said. She pinched my arm excitedly. "This is it!"

chapter sixteen

THE LAST TIME I'D LOOKED at the clock, it was nearly midnight. Now it was close to three a.m. My heart started pounding. This was it.

We sneaked out the back door and hurried downstairs. We hesitated at the alley. None of us had ever been through there at night. It was Lakey who finally said, "Come on. We've been down this alley millions of times."

The alley was still, and every shadow seemed as if it could hold a mass murderer. We stole through it, keeping close to the brick wall of our building. I was both scared and thrilled. When we got to the street, Marilyn looked around. "To tell the truth, I don't know where his car is," she said quietly. "He must

have moved it when he went out for cigarettes."

"Well, we've got to look for it, then," I said. "It can't be that far away." We walked to the block to our right but didn't see it. Then we circled around until we were to the left of our building. We saw a man walking down the street, and Marilyn whispered, "Hide!"

We rushed into a foyer and pressed against a wall so the man wouldn't see us. What if he was a murderer? This was only the fourth time in my life I'd been out this late. I couldn't remember ever being this scared. My throat got so dry, I could hardly swallow. I wanted to be back home, where I was safe. Then I thought about how we should attack the man if he wanted to kill us: Marilyn and I should jump on him, and Lakey and Maddie could kick him. Then we'd have to run, but where would we go? Then I thought I was being paranoid.

We waited, and waited, and waited, my mind in an argument with itself: *Should I be scared or not?* Finally, Marilyn peeked out. "Run!" she cried. We all ran after her. I ran as fast as I could until I realized I wa leaving Maddie behind. Then I waited for her ar took her hand. If the man wanted to hurt any of u wanted it to be me, not Maddie.

"There's Mack's car!" Marilyn screamed.

She fumbled with the keys while I watched the man down the way walking in a perfectly normal fashion. Then he went into a building.

I let myself relax as we slipped into the car and locked the doors, but then as Marilyn started trying to get out of the parking space, I felt nervous all over again. The space seemed big enough, but Marilyn had to go back and forth, back and forth, to get out. I was sure one of the neighbors would hear and call the police.

Marilyn was getting flustered. "I know you can do it, Mare," I told her.

"I have trouble judging the right side," Marilyn said. Her voice was high and childlike. "Also the back." For a moment I thought she was going to cry. Then she took a big breath, backed up again, and pulled out slowly. I couldn't watch. The car seemed like it was as big as a house. I had no idea how people could judge the back side.

"Yay, Marilyn," Lakey said from the backseat.

"Great job, Marilyn," I said from the passenger side.

"It was, wasn't it?" Marilyn said with a grin. And off we went. The street was barren, just like it was on the way to the hospital that night in the taxi. Then a car approached from the opposite direction. I was so

shocked when I saw it was a police car that I almost threw up. But it just slowly drove by.

I felt like I couldn't breathe right and cracked open my window to feel the lukewarm air. It was actually a beautiful night to run away. Marilyn pulled to the side of the road and stopped the car.

"What is it?" I said.

She breathed deeply several times. "I thought that police car was coming for us."

"Me too," the three of us said all at the same time.

Marilyn rested her head on the steering wheel. "Running away is a little stressful," she said.

"I'll say," I said. "I didn't expect it to be like this." I wondered whether my mother had felt stressed when she ran away from Pierre and Mr. Bronson with us.

But Lakey was beaming. "I think it's fun," she said, hanging over the front seat. She pulled Marilyn's head over and kissed her cheek.

Marilyn and I both turned to Maddie. She actually looked better than Marilyn. I ruffled her hair and said, "Put on your seat belt."

"You too, Lakey," Marilyn said.

"It's already on."

Marilyn seemed more confident after that, until we came to the expressway.

"Wish me luck!" she said, leaning forward over the steering wheel.

The expressway was surprisingly busy. A couple of people honked at her, and one screamed out, "Pedal to the metal!"

Marilyn got so upset, she had to pull onto the shoulder and take more deep breaths.

"Are you okay?" I said.

"I just need to breathe for a minute."

"Those were just stupid, mean people. I didn't notice anything wrong that you did."

"Really?"

"Really," I said.

"Then why did they honk?"

"Some people have nothing better to do. They're just rude and they can't help acting rude. It's like a tic. Remember that man we saw once who kept twitching his face?"

Marilyn nodded but remained on the side of the road. Then she said, "The fathers are all going to be worried."

"They'll know we're okay. They'll know we're all together."

"I left a note," Maddie squeaked.

"You what! When did you do that?" I demanded.

"I woke up and did it."

"What did you say?"

"I said we were running away."

"That's okay," Marilyn said. "They'll figure it out for themselves even without a note. Did you say where we were going, sweetie?"

"No."

"Good. You did good." Marilyn looked worriedly over her shoulder. "You wouldn't think there'd be so much traffic at this hour." She took several big breaths. "I've never driven this far before, and never on the expressway. It seems like all the cars are following me."

"Marilyn, if you can't do it, then we have to go back," I said. Then I thought I should have kept my mouth shut instead of guilt-tripping her. It was only that I really, really wanted us to get away tonight.

Marilyn kept taking big breaths. Then she lifted her head high. "Okay, I'm going to do it," she said, enunciating carefully. "I just needed to recover for a second." Our mother had taught us to always say "to," so we almost never said "gonna" but rather "going to." We also tried to say "yes" instead of "yeah." We'd actually had speech lessons for a couple of months.

What was I doing thinking about speech lessons while we were running away? Marilyn set her jaw, a lot like the way I'd seen our mother do when she felt determined about something.

Our mother had taught us so well that we thought about her rules even when she wasn't here. Even her eventual death by old age was planned with vanity. She said she wanted to be cremated as soon as possible so nobody could see her dead. "Just throw me in the ocean," she'd told us.

Marilyn was concentrating so hard on driving, I didn't think it was a good idea for any of us to talk. Anyway, I couldn't think of anything to say. I mean, I knew we should have been planning whatever it was you were supposed to plan when you ran away, but all I could think about was the present moment. Marilyn hunched forward clutching the steering wheel. Lakey and Maddie were sitting quietly. I turned around and saw that they were actually sleeping. Maddie's head fell forward. Lakey was sleeping with her head against the window. I noticed a hole in the back window and wondered if it could actually be a bullet hole. After all, it was Mack's car.

"What are the girls doing?" Marilyn said.

"Sleeping."

"Sometimes I wish I were young again," Marilyn said.

"You're not exactly old." I looked at her.

"I know. I just mean it would be nice to sleep in back while somebody else drove."

"I'll stay up for as long as you can drive."

"Thanks, sweetie," she said.

But I must have broken my promise because the next thing I knew, it was getting light and Marilyn was drinking coffee. She must have stopped for coffee while I dozed. "I'm sorry," I said. "I meant to stay awake. Are you tired?"

"I'm okay." She shrugged.

"Were you lonely without anyone awake?"

"I'm always lonely."

I studied her face. "What do you mean?"

"I don't know. I guess it's that I always have to be in charge."

This was the first time I realized what a burden we must be to Marilyn. We three younger sisters all felt that Marilyn was the responsible one. Though I was officially responsible for Maddie, in the en everything really came down to Marilyn. She was eve more responsible for us than our mother, and s was only sixteen. Like the time Maddie fell on a

in the driveway and needed stitches, it was Marilyn who had to call a taxi and figure out what doctor to take her to.

"Give me the rest of your coffee and I promise I'll stay awake."

She handed me her cup, and I noticed there was another cup between her legs. I took a drink.

"Blech," I said. "Blech. Why do people drink this?" But I took another sip. And after a few more gulps I felt like I could jump to the moon. When I finished the cup, I said, "Let's stop. I need a walk. Say, what do you think the fathers are doing right now? Isn't it funny that they're all together and we're not even there? Do you think they're up yet? Here's a field—I have to use the restroom, what about you?"

Marilyn glanced at me. "How badly do you have to go?"

"On a scale of one to ten, I guess it's a six-point-five. Hey, this coffee is great. I mean, it tastes terrible, but I'm wide awake. I think I could walk to Larry's cabin. Maybe I could even run." I tipped the cup to get the last few drops. I felt like I wanted to lick the cup. "Can you believe people used to cross the country with horses? Those poor horses. I wonder what my goat is doing. I hope he's still there when I get back."

Marilyn glanced at me curiously. "I think you've had enough coffee."

"What do you mean?"

"You're getting too hyper."

"Me? Hyper? Have you thought about what we should eat? When are we going to stop for breakfast? If it's not too long from now, I can wait to use the restroom."

"When the girls get up, we'll think about a restaurant. Nothing fancy. We just want to feed ourselves without spending too much of our stash."

"Okay, I can wait. Marilyn, do you really, really feel lonely? I mean, all the boys at your school like you, and your girlfriends always want you to hang around with them. How can you feel lonely?"

"I don't know. I think it's kind of like the way Mom feels lonely."

Someone honked, and when he drove by, he cried out, "Get her off the road!" I looked at the speedometer; we were going forty.

"Jerk," I said. "What do you mean Mom feels lonely?"

"She never told me. I just think it's true. Like, she doesn't have any friends."

"But you have friends."

"I know, but I don't know if they're true friends. We just hang around. You and the girls are my closest friends."

"I know what you mean."

"But you have your friend Nancy."

That was true. Nancy was my best friend at school. If there was a party, we always went together, and we always sat and talked together at lunch. "Yes, she's a real friend," I said. I had never thought about it before. I had one close friend at school, and Marilyn had half the class clamoring for her company. So it was strange to think of her as lonely and me as not.

"Mom is lonely too."

"No, she's not!" I said. "She goes out almost every night."

"But she doesn't have any friends, she just has boyfriends."

That was too much for me. "You're wrong. She could have all the friends she wanted if she wasn't so busy."

Marilyn shrugged and didn't say more. I watched my leg as I twitched it up and down. Boy, coffee was powerful stuff. I felt like Supergirl. We were really doing this. We were running away. I opened my window all the way, which I usually did when I was in a car. The warm, early-morning air pounded my face. I thought about my mother and the scars she would have on her face. It was an important place to have scars. If I'd broken my nose when the shopping cart crashed on me, I would feel self-conscious about my nose.

I wished I could fly. But what I was doing didn't seem that different from what I figured flying would be like, the air whipping my face, the ground speeding by. We were still in Illinois. Almost a year ago exactly we'd been on this very same stretch of highway with our mother.

As rush hour kicked into gear, more traffic appeared, and Marilyn slowed down even more. I closed my window and leaned back against my seat. I didn't think my mother was lonely at all. She was too busy for that. And even when she wasn't out with some guy, she was thinking about him. So she was busy whether she was going out or not.

Marilyn remained glued to the steering wheel, leaning forward tensely, as we went about thirty miles per hour. I wanted to complain that at this rate we'd spend a month on the road, unless we got pulled over by the highway patrol first. But I didn't say anything because I didn't want to make her more nervous.

Lakey said, "Where are we?"

I turned back to look at her. "You're awake," I said.

"I just woke up. Are we there yet?"

"We're just about to cross over into Iowa," I said. "Say, I wonder how my goat is doing. I got really attached to him. He follows me around, but Jiro doesn't want him in the house. He's smarter than you might think a goat would be. He has a stuffed animal that he takes everywhere, like a teddy bear. Do you think he's doing okay without me?"

I saw Marilyn and Lakey lock eyes in the rearview mirror. "She drank some coffee," Marilyn said. So I tried to shut up, but it was hard. I started shaking my leg again instead. I took out some of Jiro's gum and started chewing it like a T. rex chewing a liver.

"Gum anyone?" I said.

"No thanks," they both said.

"Jiro makes really cool gum. He makes it so the taste lasts longer. You know how gum loses its taste so fast? I tried timing it once, and it's true that when you chew his gum, the taste really does last longer. One of his customers says he deserves to be as rich as the Wrigleys. I can't stop talking," I said.

In one hour I chewed all five packs of gum I'd

brought. At one point I had seven pieces in my mouth at once.

The sun was fully up by the time Maddie woke up. We bought snacks and used the bathroom at a gas stop, then filed back to the car and got settled in again, driving for hours and hours. Marilyn eventually got comfortable enough behind the wheel to go faster on the open highway. By late in the afternoon, we'd made it through all of Iowa, singing every song we knew and playing countless rounds of Why? with Maddie to keep her distracted.

Finally, Marilyn said, "I have to go to sleep. Everybody keep your eyes open for a cheap motel." There were approximately one zillion cheap motels, so it didn't take long to find one.

chapter seventeen

WE ENDED UP IN EASTERN Nebraska in extended-stay accommodations, the kind of place where some people lived for months at a time. Old men sat around outside chain-smoking, the smoke billowing from their noses as if they could not be bothered to put their mouths through the effort of opening. One man spit about once every thirty seconds. Another chomped a wad of gum as big as a plum. Every so often he concentrated on blowing huge bubbles that the other men watched with interest and occasional admiration. After an especially big bubble one or the other would nod and say, "Uh-huh, brother," or "Good one, there, boy."

When we went into the office to pay, the manager seemed surprised.

"We don't get many young ladies here," he said. "Not many Orientals, either."

"Is it dangerous?" I asked.

"No, but we got a lot of men here. And they got some rough edges."

"As long as it's not dangerous," I said.

"Oh, no. But they spit and such. Sometimes they spit tobacco. It's not pretty."

Our room was dim even after we turned on the lights, and the two-burner gas stove was marred with streaks and drops of dried brown gunk. Near the stove was a little basket holding several razor blades. A faded note read *If you spill anything sticky, make sure to scrape it off.* Scraped-off dried brown gunk lined the edges of a couple of the blades. Another small sign, on the wall near the stove, read IF YOU ARE DRUNK, PLEASE USE HEAT WITH CARE.

Marilyn took out a cigarette and tried to light it on the burner. The flame leaped up, and I smelled burnt hair.

None of us even undressed. We just plopped down on the bed and fell asleep. Our sleep schedule was all messed up, and we ended up waking around two a.m.

Lakey got up first and woke the rest of us. I heard crickets singing happily all around. Our mother used to shake her head at the chirping of crickets. "It's all about procreating, girls," she'd say. "That whole racket you hear."

When we walked out to leave, three old men were sitting outside, one of them asleep right there in the chair. I recognized them from earlier. They must have spent their entire lives sitting outside talking and sleeping. I could feel the two awake men watching me as I walked to the office and dropped the key to the room in the mail slot. They scratched their noses, smoked their cigarettes, blew their bubbles, scratched their chests, and just generally shifted their eyes among the four of us like we were scenes on a television set.

Once inside the car, I saw that a pick-up was parked perpendicular to ours and was sticking out a bit. I knew Marilyn would have trouble getting out of the space.

"Shelby, can you get out and tell me if I'm too close to the pick-up?"

So I got out and watched. "Stop!" I cried out. "Stop, Marilyn!" I waved my arms in the air.

She opened her window. "What is it?"

"You're going to be about an inch away if you keep going."

"An inch is fine. As long as I don't hit it."

"It only looks like an inch to me. It might be less," I said. I felt the eyes of the old men on us. A light turned on in the office. "Marilyn, hurry!"

"How can I hurry when you say I'm an inch away?"

She brought the car slightly forward and to the right. Then she jumped the curb and my heart stopped. Fortunately, she stopped right away and didn't go far. I walked to the window. "Are you okay?" I asked.

"No, but I have to do this. There's no other choice."

"Do you want me to try?"

"No, I'm going to do it because I have to."

So I stood by watching as she backed up again.

"About three inches!" I called excitedly.

She backed up slowly. The men outside clapped. The third one had woken up and was also watching. The motel manager had stepped out in his pajamas. I felt my face grow hot. We weren't very competent at running away.

Once the car was free, I got back in. Marilyn

looked like she was going to be ill. But she was a stronger person than I'd thought, not that I didn't think she was a strong person, but I think I thought that she wasn't especially strong and that maybe she didn't think she was strong at all. That's what I thought at that moment, anyway. She put the car in forward and drove off. She looked at me and said, "Mom says never let it bother you when a man stares at you."

"Yeah, but they weren't staring at you because you're pretty," I said. "That's what she meant."

"That's not what she said," Marilyn answered.

We made our way back toward the highway in silence, the car creeping along in the dark. I turned around to check on my sisters, who had been wide-eyed and silent throughout all of this. Maddie looked terrified. I wondered whether she was even more scared of us right now than of Mr. Bronson. "Sweetie," I said to Maddie. "Sweetie pie." I took off my seat belt and reached in back to stroke her cheek.

She burst into tears. "I'm scared!"

"Why don't you ride in back, Shelby," Marilyn suggested.

She pulled over, and Lakey and I traded places. "Maddie, let's play Why?" I said.

She was quiet for a moment, then squeaked out, "Why?"

"Because it's a fun game."

"Why?"

"Because, uh, because I like it."

"Why?"

"Because you like it," I said.

She smiled a little at that. "Why?"

"Why do you like it? You're the only one who knows."

"It's fun," she said. "Why?"

"I don't know," I said. "Game over."

"Let's find a grocery store. I'm starving," Marilyn said.

"We could just go to a restaurant," I said.

"We're saving money, remember? Anyway, what restaurant would be open at this hour?"

"Denny's."

"I'll tell you what, if we see a Denny's first, we'll go there; if we see a grocery store first, we'll go there."

Right at the edge of town, Marilyn spotted lights. "Hey look! There's a grocery store." She pulled into the nearly deserted parking lot.

"Should we bring all our money?" I asked her.

"We better—we shouldn't leave it in the car."

Maddie said, "I'm scared to go out this late."

Lakey added, "Me too."

For all I knew, we were already wanted by the FBI, or whoever looked for runaways. I imagined our faces on a wanted flyer. I felt like the one time I went skiing with my friend Nancy's family. I'd felt excited and scared at the same time, like I did and didn't want to ski down the hill below me.

Marilyn took both Lakey's and Maddie's hands and walked across the parking lot with me following. I kept my hand in a pocket to protect my money. I closed my eyes and tried to calm down, but with my eyes closed, I saw a police officer arresting us. I opened my eyes. I was a big mess inside. I was sure everybody in the world was looking for us.

Once when my mother was dating the owner of a health food store, he put us all on niacin, which made my whole face tingle. Right now the cool air-conditioning hitting my face as the automatic door slid open made my cheeks tingle. Even my face was nervous.

The cashier looked at us with open surprise. Marilyn hardly glanced at him, just got a cart and began wheeling. The girls turned to me to hold hands. We walked into the produce section. I felt eyes on me and turned around to see a security guard and the cashier standing nearby. They pretended to be checking out some coconuts as Marilyn filled a plastic bag with apples.

"I guess oranges, too," I said.

"Okay," Marilyn said. "Anything you girls want? How about yogurt?"

"It might spoil in the car," I said.

"Yeah, I guess crackers and cheese would be better. You look like you're going to be sick, Shelby."

"What if the police are already looking for us?" I said in a low voice.

Maddie cried out, "It's the middle of the night!"

The security man said, "Is there anything we can help you with?"

"No, thanks," Marilyn replied firmly. "We know how to shop."

We walked to the cracker aisle and got four boxes of Ak-Mak flatbread, which was made from whole wheat. Our mother made us eat Ak-Mak whenever we wanted crackers. She would buy four boxes, so we each had our own.

We also got cheese, bread, tuna fish, sardines (which our mother thought had magical health qualities), mayonnaise, Coke for Marilyn, instant coffee, a jug of distilled water, and paper cups.

I didn't really feel so nervous any longer. In fact, it was kind of fun to be shopping in the middle of the night. But Maddie still seemed terrified. She squeezed my hand hard. When we got to the checkout aisle, the cashier was watching the security guard talking to a man who looked drunk—he could barely stand straight. One year when my mother decided she wanted to develop her mind, she bought a subscription to *Psychology Today,* and I read an article about how the dead of night was a frontier to some people, similar to the way the western United States had once been a frontier. You learned a lot when you had a mother like ours. So here we were on the vast frontier, shopping.

The cashier said, "Running away?" and smiled at Marilyn.

For a second she looked stricken, and then she smiled in return. "Right," Marilyn said. "We're going to the Bahamas if you want to come."

"I wish," he said.

As we walked back to the car, I noticed that Maddie's cut-offs had grown soaked—she'd wet her pants. When we got to the car, I said, "Sweetie, don't worry, we'll change your pants."

Marilyn dug through the trunk for new pants and underwear for Maddie. We got her changed and

Marilyn said, "Shelby, stay in back with her."

"Maddie, do you want me to keep sitting in back with you?" I said.

She didn't answer for a few moments, and then she nodded.

"Do you want me to sit in the middle?" I asked. Sometimes she liked that.

"No, thank you," she said. "Does anyone mind if I crack the window?"

"Of course not," I said. "Are you hot? I'll open mine, too."

"You don't have to," she said. "I don't want to bother you."

"Maddie, it doesn't bother me."

But she didn't say anything more.

Marilyn looked at me in the rearview mirror. "I don't feel guilty for getting you away from Mr. Bronson," she suddenly said to Maddie.

Lakey piped up. "I hope he croaks."

"Lakey!" Marilyn said. "It's bad luck to say things like that."

"I don't believe in bad luck," Lakey said. "I hope he croaks."

I said, "What if we grow up and have kids just like us?" Everybody laughed except Maddie. Marilyn handed each of us a box of Ak-Mak and one package of cheese. I ripped open my food and couldn't stop eating until there was only one cracker left in the box.

Marilyn hunkered over the steering wheel. But once we got going on the highway, she sped up to fifty miles an hour. That was a positive sign.

For the next several hours, I took off my glasses and stuck my head out the window for as long as I could stand it. When we passed the first sign that pointed us toward Colorado, Lakey shouted out, "We're almost there!" I knew we still had a ways to go, but with the wind hitting my face, I felt like nothing could happen to us as long as we were all together. But I also knew I'd felt the same way before my mother's accident. I rolled up my window at last and leaned back in my seat. I put my glasses back on and felt my tangled mess of hair. My mother always made me carry a comb when we traveled. But she wasn't here. Even though I thought that Marilyn and I were the grown-ups, maybe Marilyn thought I was one of the kids. That would make her the only grown-up and even lonelier than she already felt.

I slept restlessly. I dreamed I was reaching, reaching, my arms stretched out in front of me, reaching so desperately that my muscles ached, blood pouring out of the ache, and then I was on the beach, the sand sparkling. Then, awake; or maybe not. Driving in the dark. The stars like flashes of the dream I could no longer remember. Reaching. For something. Except there was no dream now, so I was left with *reaching*. Awake. Asleep. Awake. Asleep. Awake. The more I reached the more I ached. And finally the ache became this: These were some of the best years of my life. Right here. Now. Maybe Mr. Bronson was right, and the future would hurt me. But I wanted it anyway. That was something Mr. Bronson wouldn't understand. An explosion of lights to the south: a factory, lit by fluorescent lights on a flat plain. For some reason I felt pure happiness wash over me at the sight. The explosion of lights seemed like a miracle. I wanted to see Mr. Bronson so I could tell him what that felt like. Then I was dreaming again. . . .

When I next woke up, a cigarette hung from Marilyn's mouth. She took it out and flicked it over the ashtray. I imagined all that smoke whirling down into her lungs. I wondered whether she was destined to be like our mother, living in the universe where beauty meant everything.

"What are you looking at?" Marilyn asked.

"Nothing," I said.

An ash flew backward and landed on my shirt. But I didn't say anything, because if she had to smoke, she had to smoke.

I looked at the map we'd bought at a gas stop in Illinois. "We can make it into Colorado today. But I don't know how far we'll get before you'll need to sleep again."

"I feel fine."

"Denver's still hours away."

"Let's have some coffee."

We filled a couple of paper cups with water and instant coffee. "Hold your breath and it won't be so bad," Marilyn advised me.

I held my breath and glugged down the mixture, including the ground coffee. Oh, man. Oh—man—oh—man—oh—man. Once you breathed, it tasted wickedly awful. I ate my last cracker. Maddie was eating her cheese, meticulously tearing off one string at a time.

She leaned on me. "Can we buy a house?" she asked.

"For three thousand dollars, we can't even buy a barn," Marilyn said. "Plus, you don't have your money, so we don't even have three thousand."

"I hope Mr. Bronson croaks," Lakey said.

"Stop saying that," Marilyn scolded.

"Really?" Maddie pulled at my hair. "Really we can't buy a house?" I hardly dared to breathe. She was pulling my hair! Only my Maddie pulled my hair. I was ready to let her pull it all out if she needed to. But she gave it one last tug and looked directly at me. "*Really* we can't?" she asked again.

"Really," I said. I was silent for a moment. Then I said, "I hope they don't tell Mom that we're missing. It'll only make her worried."

"I was thinking about that," Marilyn said. "But we had no choice. If we're going to be together, we had to leave."

Nebraska was so flat, we sang Bruce Springsteen's "Badlands," except we changed the words to match the terrain: *Flatlands, you gotta live it every day, let the broken hearts stand, as the price you've gotta pay.*

When we finished the chorus, we fell apart because nobody knew the words. Instead, we kept singing the chorus over and over. Boy, did we sound bad. Suddenly, Maddie was laughing hysterically. That made me laugh, and then Marilyn and Lakey started laughing.

By the time we crossed the border into Burlington, Colorado, around noon, Marilyn and I were practically drunk on coffee. We resorted to our store of memorized songs, singing "Ninety-nine Bottles of Beer on the Wall" at the top of our lungs and "Puff the Magic Dragon" for about an hour. Then we got lost for another hour trying to avoid the midday traffic heading to Denver.

"Where did they put Interstate 70?" Marilyn kept saying. Then she decided to take Interstate 25 because 70 seemed to have disappeared. *Then* we found a rinky-dink highway and headed west.

Once I knew we were going in the right direction toward Larry's cabin, I studied Marilyn's profile carefully from the backseat for signs of fatigue. It was late afternoon by now, and she'd been driving for twelve straight hours, with only short gas station breaks to stretch her legs. "Why don't we find another motel, Mare? You've got to be exhausted by now."

But she just glanced at me in the rearview mirror and smiled over at Lakey. "Really, I feel fine. In fact, I'm really wired now that I know we're so close. Let's just keep going, okay? I promise you guys I'll stop if I get too tired." And we were all so anxious to get there, we didn't argue any further.

When we at last reached Montezuma, Colorado, around dinnertime, Lakey cried out, "This is it! We're in the right town. I know exactly how to get to the cabin."

"How are we going to get *into* the cabin?" Maddie asked out of the blue. Nobody spoke at first. How had we not considered that?

"We'll have to figure that out when we get there," I finally said. "We may have to break a window, but we can pay Larry back later."

"Do we have enough money for a window?" Maddie asked.

"Yes," I said. "We could buy a lot of windows."

"Hmm," Lakey said. "I don't know *exactly* how to get there from here, but I know how to get there once we find his road. The road is called Mountain View. And his cabin is above an Indian reservation."

Marilyn stopped for gas. We'd been using full-service stations so far, but I guess the thought of paying for broken windows got her worried about money again, so we filled up the tank by ourselves. All four of us got out and stared at the whatever it was called—the big thing that held the gas hose.

"How do we make it go?" Maddie said.

"It can't be too complicated," Marilyn said. "I mean, even stupid people can do it, so I'm sure we can."

I opened the little door on our gas tank and unscrewed the cap.

Marilyn put the hose in, but nothing happened. Finally, the man who worked there came out. "Can I help you young ladies?"

"We need gas," Marilyn said crisply.

"You got money? You have to pay first."

"We do? Okay, here's five dollars." She reached into her purse, trying to hide the contents from the man. "By the way, do you know where Mountain View Road is?"

"Yep, it's that road right over there."

"We just came from that direction," I said. "We're a little confused because we don't have much experience." Marilyn shot me the evil stink eye to shut me up.

A few minutes later we were gassed up and heading down Mountain View Road on our way to our new life as runaways. It was almost too easy. Once we reached Larry's cabin, we'd be made in the shade. There were no addresses anywhere, but there was only one house on Mountain View as far as we could see. "I recognize the trees in the yard," Lakey said excitedly. Maddie, Lakey, and I screamed as Marilyn pulled in the driveway.

We got out and peered into one of the windows in front. All we could see inside was murky dimness. I looked at Lakey. "Is this it?"

"It looks like it might be," she said.

"What do you mean, it looks like it might be?" I said.

"It looks like it might be," she said again.

"All right. Let's figure out how to get in."

We tried the front door, just in case, but of course it was locked. We found a screwdriver in the trunk of the car, but we couldn't figure out what to do with it. Marilyn pried at the lock, but nothing happened. We tried the back door and every window.

"We might need to break a window after all," Marilyn said. "We should have brought goggles or something. What if the glass goes flying?"

We decided that Marilyn should break in because she was the oldest and probably also the strongest. "There's a bunch of fallen branches," I said, pointing to the ground. I handed one to Marilyn. She tried swinging it and shook her head.

"It isn't exactly right," she said.

So I found another one. It was nearly twice as thick as the last one and certainly appeared to be the perfect branch for breaking a window. But Marilyn tried swinging it and said it was too heavy for her to swing it hard enough.

We went through three more branches before Marilyn found the perfect window-bashing branch.

She put on three sweatshirts plus another three over her head, so if the glass went flying, it wouldn't cut her. I guided her to the window and she lifted the branch. I held her hands and showed her where she should hit. Then Maddie, Lakey, and I stepped back.

"Okay," I called out.

She swung—a direct hit! We all screamed. The glass cracked but didn't break. We all groaned. "One more time in the same place," I encouraged her. She hit the window again, and glass fell inside, a few shards flying toward her. Boy, she would be good with a piñata. Maddie, Lakey, and I cheered. Marilyn peeled off all the sweatshirts on her head and looked with satisfaction at the window. Using the branch, she pushed in the last of the glass. Then we all stood still and stared at one another.

"I'll go first," Lakey finally offered.

We hoisted her up and she jumped inside. She looked out the window at us. "It's the wrong one."

"The wrong what?" Maddie, Marilyn, and I said at the same time.

"The wrong house."

"The wrong house? Are you sure?" Marilyn asked.

"Yes."

I said accusingly, "I thought you said it looked like Larry's house."

"It does look like Larry's house," Lakey replied defensively. "But it's not."

She climbed back out. "Well, we need to leave some money for the broken window," I said. "How much does a window cost?"

Nobody knew. "Let's just leave a hundred," Marilyn said. "That's twenty-five dollars each, but Maddie doesn't have her money, so it's thirty-three apiece."

We took out our money and gave some to Marilyn. She leaned into the window and dropped the money inside.

"Now what?" Lakey said.

Marilyn said, "We'll have to stay at a motel until we can decide what to do." She looked at Lakey. "Unless you still think you can find his house."

"It's around here somewhere. I remember we had

to drive a long way to get to it for the wedding. Maybe we should take the road up farther."

We got back in the car, throwing our branch into the passenger side with Lakey. After we'd gone a little way, I said, "Well, does it look familiar?"

Marilyn snapped, "Stop pressuring her, she's trying."

"I'm not pressuring her, I'm just trying to figure out where this cabin is."

"All right, let's just drive a little more and see," Marilyn said.

We followed the road until the odometer said we'd gone one and a half miles. Lakey called out, "There it is! I think that's it!"

So we got out, and Lakey studied the cabin.

"Why did you say, 'I *think* that's it'?" I asked.

"It looks the way I remember." She walked around the house as we all followed. Then she spotted something and walked toward the backyard. "This is definitely it," she said.

"How do you know?" I said.

"Because I touched that tree over there and made a wish.

I walked over to where she was standing.

I turned to Marilyn for a verdict.

"All right," she said. "But this is the last window I'm going to break. I can't be breaking every window we come across."

Rewrapped in all the sweatshirts, Marilyn slammed our branch against one of the side windows. Lakey crawled into the window, chanting "This is it" the whole time. After she got inside, she triumphantly repeated, "This is it! I told you I recognized it. I'll open the door for you."

We went around to the front door, and she let us in. It was a lovely cabin, with flowered curtains. I couldn't imagine Larry with flowered curtains. His new wife must have hung them up.

"I told you I knew where it was," Lakey said.

The phone started ringing, and we all froze. "It's my dad," Lakey said. "I can just feel it."

"Don't answer!" Marilyn said. We all stood around staring at the phone until it finally stopped ringing.

We couldn't find a can opener in the cabin. And we couldn't get the mayonnaise jar open. So we ate crackers, sardines, and oranges. The crackers seemed as good as any cracker anywhere, anytime. "Who doesn't have a can opener in their house?" I said.

"It's a cabin, not a house," Lakey said.

"Well, we need to buy a can opener," I said. "Shall we all drive back to town together, or should someone stay here?"

"We should all go together!" Maddie cried out. "I don't want to separate!"

"Don't worry, nobody's going to leave you," I said.

Marilyn said, "I think we've had enough stress for one day."

The phone rang again, and we stayed perfectly still, as if whoever was on the line would know we were there if we moved.

Larry had a VCR and a shelf of movies. We let Maddie pick the movie, and she chose *Alien*. "Are you sure?" I said. "It's scary."

"Yes, I like alien movies."

"Maddie, you're going to be scared later," I said.

"Pluhthegeeeease," she said. "Pluhthegeeeease."

"Okay," Marilyn said.

We watched the movie, eating our crackers like popcorn. We pulled blankets off of the beds and all sat together on the floor.

Maddie clung to me during the scary parts, and Lakey clung to Marilyn. When the movie ended, Maddie said, "I'm scared. I think we should go to a motel."

"That would cost money. We can stay here for free," Marilyn said.

Maddie said, "Pluhthegeeeease. Pluhthegeeease."

I could tell Marilyn was considering it, but in the end she said, "No, we need to save our money."

Maddie clung to me in bed, and every so often she would say, "Did you hear that?"

"I didn't hear anything," I kept saying.

Finally, she went to sleep and Marilyn and Lakey went to sleep, and I was awake alone. Even though hours had passed since I drank my last cup of coffee, I still felt hyper. All of a sudden I heard noises that I hadn't noticed before. The wind made a *woooo* sound, and something seemed to be scurrying outside. I could hear every little thing through the broken window. We needed to get that fixed first thing tomorrow. We were out here in the middle of nowhere. I got up and went into the kitchen and found a big knife. Then I put it under the bed where I was sleeping. I would have put it under the pillow, but I didn't want to accidentally cut my head off. Wow, I was surprised that coffee was legal.

Finally, I couldn't keep myself up, even with the strange noises I kept hearing. I fell asleep and dreamed that Mr. Bronson had discovered us. Then I heard Maddie calling, "Shelby. Shelby." And I was awake.

"What?" I said. It was still dark out.

"I need to go to the bathroom. Will you come with me?"

"Sure." I didn't tell her that I was scared too. But I grabbed the knife.

"What's that for?" Maddie said.

"In case I need to protect us."

"Okay, that's what I thought."

Walking through the hallway with my knife, I knew that I would do anything to keep my Maddie from getting hurt. It was just one door down the hall, but you never knew what might happen.

Then we got back in bed and Maddie said, "Will you stay up until I fall back to sleep?"

"Okay," I said. "Maddie?"

"What?"

"Are you okay?"

"What do you mean?"

"Are you glad you came?"

"Uh-huh," she said. "It's fun to run away. It's like going camping."

She fell asleep again. I closed my eyes and could see parts of the movie as clearly as if I were watching it. Then I felt scared again.

The next morning I was the last one up. My sisters

were dressed and walking through the house making a list of what we needed to do or buy:

1. Fix window
2. Can opener
3. Ak-Mak
4. Popcorn
5. Peach yogurt
6. Another big knife (for Marilyn)
7. Shampoo

"Can you think of anything else, Shelby?" Marilyn asked.

"I was thinking we need a cat," I said.

"A cat?" my sisters said in unison.

"We need a pet."

"For what? Then we'll have to pay for cat food," Marilyn said.

The phone started ringing again, and we all stayed still and quiet. When it stopped ringing, we relaxed again.

"Do we need dishwashing soap? Regular soap? And detergent?" I said.

"Okay, bath soap. There's enough dishwashing liquid and detergent to last until the end of time," Marilyn said. "Anything else?"

"I don't think so," I said. "Except a cat."

"No pet," Marilyn said. "Maybe later we can get one."

So we all piled into the car and drove around until we found a grocery store. This time we weren't scared at all. In fact, we walked into the store as confident as we'd been since before our mother had her accident.

When we got back to the cabin, we unpacked our bags. I noticed Maddie had packed a thick book.

"What did you bring that for?" I asked.

"Mr. Bronson got it for me. It's about manners for young ladies. He said I had to memorize it."

I randomly opened up the book. A young lady never laughs in a loud manner. It is more appropriate to laugh in a lighthearted but quiet manner. It's vulgar to show your teeth while laughing. "I didn't know laughing was so complicated! I don't think you need manners like that when you run away," I said.

"Blech," Marilyn said. "He got you that book?"

"You don't think I might need it?"

"No," I said. "I think we should destroy it."

"Me too," Marilyn said.

"Me too," Lakey said.

"Let's burn it!" I said.

So we found some matches and took the book outside. We put a lot of sticks inside and on top of the book, and then Marilyn lit a match. It took nearly the whole box of matches to get a good fire going. We weren't really nature girls. If we were, we probably would have burned it faster. Finally, flames shot up out of the book and we watched the burning paper shrivel up. The cover was a bit harder to burn. We found some newspaper inside to keep the fire hot so that we could destroy the cover. The heat felt good against my face.

"Let's hold hands and twirl," Lakey said.

"Around the fire!" Maddie said.

"But we could burn ourselves," I said.

We all looked at Marilyn. "Okay, we'll twirl around the fire, but be careful."

We twirled as fast as we could around the fire. The wind blew, spreading ash and embers everywhere, and we had to stomp on some leaves and embers. For a second there we were losing the battle, and I worried we were going to start a forest fire. But after a while there were no more embers, and the book was gone.

I pounded my chest. "For we are the all-powerful daughters of Helen Kimura!"

Maddie pounded her chest and said, "For we are powerful girls!"

We went inside to eat and to plan our new life.

"I guess I should get a job," Marilyn said between bites of cracker. "But there's no hurry. Since we don't pay rent, we won't be spending a lot of money."

"Maybe we should make a budget," I said.

Marilyn said, "If we spend ten dollars or so a day on food, that's . . . uh . . . uh . . ."

"Maybe two hundred days," Lakey said.

We were still eating and planning when someone knocked on the door. We didn't move until we heard "This is Deputy Jensen. Come on, girls. Your fathers are looking for you." We looked at one another. A man peeked through the broken window. "Girls? I can see you. Don't make me climb through this window. Your fathers are on their way here. They called the station. They're coming to get you, and you can make it a lot easier on yourselves if you come to the station with me and wait for them."

We looked to Marilyn for an answer. But what could she do? She said softly to us, "I guess we're caught."

Deputy Jensen had brought another deputy, a surly man with a huge paunch. We packed up our stuff while the paunchy guy got the keys from Marilyn and drove Tony's car away. In the squad car, the four of us crammed into the backseat. Deputy Jensen helped each of us in, as if we were honored guests. As we pulled away from the house, Maddie whispered in my ear. "My father is going to kill me."

"So is mine," I answered.

"No," she whispered. "I mean, is my father really going to kill me?"

"Of course not." But I knew Mr. Bronson would be really hard on Maddie, and I didn't think I could stop that.

"What are you talking about back there, girls?" Jensen eyed us through the rearview mirror. Nobody answered him, so he eyed me. "Which one are you?"

"Shelby."

"Well, Shelby, what are you talking about back there?"

"Ah . . . using the bathroom?"

"Are you asking me or telling me?"

"Asking. I mean, telling." Before Deputy Jensen could say anything else, the radio squawked, "We have a 371 in progress at Al's Liquor. Are you available, Carl?"

"I'll swing by there, but please send backup. I'm carrying a load vis-à-vis the 424."

"Affirmative. Uh, can you pick up something for lunch?"

"Sure. See ya."

He started his siren and we were racing down the street. "Put your seat belts on, girls."

At Al's Liquor, he ran inside with his gun drawn. In a few minutes he came out with a middle-aged woman in handcuffs. He looked at us. He looked at her. "Well, this is a little unorthodox," he said, then he sat her in front while we stayed squished together in back. The woman turned to look at us and then leaned forward and ripped off a piece of upholstery with her teeth!

"You need to settle," Jensen told her calmly.

We all glared at one another. I don't know what my sisters were thinking, but I was worried that we were going to be put in a cell with the woman. Finally I couldn't stand not knowing for sure.

"Are you going to put us in jail?" I asked.

"Not unless you want me to." What kind of answer was that? At a stop sign, he turned back to look at me. "I ought to, but your fathers might not appreciate that."

"They're going to be mad at *us*," I said.

"Yeah, and you know what? You deserve that. See, if I put you in jail, they'll be mad at me, but if I don't put you in jail, they'll be mad at you. Got that?" The car behind us honked. "Who honks at a deputy?" he said.

When we got to the station, Deputy Jensen told us that our fathers would be a few hours and we had no choice but to wait. Then he said, "I need to book her." He gestured toward the woman.

This running away business was exhausting. "I feel all spent," I said. I'd never used the word "spent" like that before, but our mother said that sometimes, putting a hand to her forehead dramatically. She might not have been teaching us the things Mr. Bronson wanted, but she was surely teaching us a lot.

Marilyn put her hand to her forehead and said, "Me too."

We sat on a bench watching another deputy cut pieces of paper in half for some reason. It probably wasn't what he'd envisioned when he'd joined the force. Deputy Jensen had gone somewhere. We could have made a break for it, but there was nowhere to go. The car keys were in a drawer—we'd seen Jensen put them there. The station was quiet and empty. Maybe the other deputies were out on patrol. Or maybe there wasn't much crime here so there weren't many deputies. The man who was cutting looked at us. "First time?" he said.

"Yes," Marilyn said. "We've never been arrested."

He nodded and then went back to his cutting.

I turned to Maddie. "How are you doing?"

"I have to use the bathroom," she said.

Marilyn asked loudly, "Excuse me, can my sister use the bathroom?"

"Sure thing," he said. "It's down that hall there to the right."

Maddie grabbed my hand. "Come with me!" she said. "I like you."

"Maddie!" I said, hugging her. "I like you too." She smiled, just a little peekaboo of a smile.

We went to the bathroom together, walking down a corridor past some high windows. I stood on tiptoe to look into one of the windows. A couple of glum-looking men looked back. I guess they were under arrest. I was glad they hadn't put us in a jail cell.

"Hold my hand," I said.

"What was in there?"

"Some people under arrest."

"I want to see!" Now, that was my Maddie talking!

I lifted her up and she said, "Wooow."

I took her hand and we went to the restroom. On the way back she wanted to see the prisoners again, so I lifted her up. "Wooow," she said again.

Back at the bench Marilyn said softly, "My father is going to kill me. First he's going to yell at me, and then he's going to kill me."

Maddie looked concerned. "Really—he'll kill you?" she said.

"Well, he'll ground me until the end of time, and that will kill me."

"I don't know what Jiro will do. Once he got mad at me for trying to run away."

"I don't know what my father will do either," Lakey said. "Probably ground me, but not until the end of time. Maybe a month."

Maddie didn't say anything, but I could almost see her returning to her Mr. Bronson personality. She literally deflated, slouching in the seat, hanging her head. "You'll be okay," I said, taking her hands. "You're going to come live with us." Marilyn gave me a look that said, *Shut up, Shelby.* But I couldn't. "Maddie's going to live with Jiro and me now. If she doesn't, I'm not going home with him. I'll . . . I'll . . . I'll kick somebody."

"Is that all we have to do?" Maddie said. "Kick somebody? Should I kick somebody too?"

"If you want," I said.

Jensen walked into the room. He nodded at us. "Just checking. Is Deputy Wilson keeping you in line?"

"Yeah," Wilson said. "It's their first time." He said that as if there would be more times.

Jensen sauntered out of the room again. The hours of just sitting there started to get to me, and I felt so tired, I could no longer keep my eyes open. It was dark by now. Maddie laid her head in my lap, and we both dozed off. Even though the seat was uncomfortable, with Maddie lying in my lap, it was easy to fall asleep.

I woke up to Marilyn shaking me. "What?" I said.

"He's gone."

"Who's gone?"

"The guy with the scissors."

"Deputy Wilson?"

"Uh-huh. Let's get out of here." Marilyn dangled the car keys in front of me. She must have taken them from the drawer!

"Where would we go?" I studied my beautiful sister's excited face.

"We can go anywhere. How about California? We loved it there. We'll get an apartment and I'll find a job."

It was tempting. But . . .

"What's wrong?" Marilyn asked.

I wasn't sure. But somehow running away again didn't make sense to me. Somehow it seemed like time to face our punishment. "I don't think we should run away again," I said. My mouth said that before my brain could catch up.

"But why not?" Marilyn said, sounding genuinely confused.

"I guess, I don't know, but I guess because Mom's always running away every time a man annoys her."

"So?"

"So we have to be different from her."

"Why would we want to be different from her?"

"Because. Because she's lonely. You said so." I stroked Maddie's wild hair. She was snoring. She sounded like a lawn mower. "And because we won't be able to take care of Maddie. Apartments in California are probably expensive."

"Then you could get a job too."

"I'm not even fourteen yet," I said. "Marilyn, we need to talk to all of the fathers together and work something out. I'll talk to them if you don't want to."

Lakey had been listening. She looked up at Marilyn. Marilyn was pursing her lips. But she didn't say more, just sat down and turned away from me. It took me a long time to fall asleep this time. I worried about what I would say to the fathers. I wanted to explain to them why we ran away. Maybe if I explained it right, they would let Maddie stay with me and Jiro. I remembered all of the times my mother ran away. From men like Pierre and men like Mr. Bronson. And others: Johnny, Maxwell, Franklin, and Andrew. Those were all I could think of off the top of my head. And every single time, when she returned, she had to face these men. I loved my mother, adored her. But after a lifetime of wanting to be like her, I realized I didn't want to be her, exactly. I didn't want to run away.

At some point I must have fallen asleep again because I woke to Larry saying, "Girls." Behind him stood the other fathers. They all looked as stern as Mr. Bronson. We jumped up. I felt scared and defiant at the same time.

Larry shook his head at us. "All right, Lakey, you and I will ride with Mack and Marilyn, and Shelby and Maddie will go with their fathers."

The fathers shook hands with Deputy Jensen and thanked him as Marilyn gently awakened Maddie. I approached the deputy. "I guess I'm sorry. I mean, I *am* sorry we bothered you."

"It's my job," he said. "But don't try it again."

"We won't," I said. "At least I doubt it." Then we meekly followed the fathers outside and all stood by the cars.

The moment the station's door closed, Bronson started in. "You girls are in a lot of trouble. Let me tell you about that." He looked at my sisters and then at me. He took a big breath, his nostrils flaring. He looked like an angry bull.

Mack said, "Now wait a second. I'm going first. I need to give them a piece of my mind. Girls, what you've done isn't just idiotness, it's the maximum of idiotness. If you took all the idiotness in the world and rolled it into one big idiot ball, this is what you would have here."

I stole a glance at Jiro. His face was unemotional.

"I'm sorry," I said to Jiro. I looked down at my sandals. They were really dirty.

He nodded, deep in thought. "You didn't mean bad," he finally said. And he patted my shoulder far more gently than I knew I deserved.

Mack cried, "What do you mean, she didn't mean bad?"

"Jiro," I pleaded. "We belong together. We're sisters." I grabbed Maddie and pulled her to me. She neither resisted nor complied. She felt so limp, I wondered how she could stand up.

"You didn't mean bad, but I have to punish," Jiro said.

"Dad," Marilyn said, turning to her father with tears in her eyes. "We've always been together, and we were separated. What happened to Mom was bad enough, but it was even worse because we were separated."

"And you took Maddie away from me," I cried. "Mom said for me to always watch out for Maddie, but how can I do that if she's away from me?"

Mack threw his hands in the air and looked at the other fathers.

Larry's voice was calm and gentle as he said, "Look, we're in uncharted territory here. We're all doing our best to cope with your mother's accident."

Jiro looked at me. "No excuse. But I understand."

Mack said, "But come on, men! In terms of an act of idiotness, this is the maximum. Marilyn doesn't even have a driver's license."

I touched Jiro's arm. "We love Maddie so much. We just wanted to do right by her. It's hard to explain, but funny stuff was happening. Like her letters didn't seem like her. They seemed like Mr. Bronson was dictating them."

Mr. Bronson didn't say anything. What could he say?

Larry said, "Let's just get everyone home."

Mr. Bronson said, "Madeline, discipline is one of

the most important parts of being a parent. I would be hurting you in the long run if I didn't punish you."

Jiro patted my shoulder. "Dangerous to run away. Many weirdo in America. Some in Japan, too, but not as many."

"I know. But we didn't know what else to do." My nose was starting to sting, like it sometimes did when I was about to cry. But I was *not* going to cry.

Mr. Bronson said, "I'm taking Madeline back home." He glared at me when he said that.

Maddie burst into tears. Jiro said, "I don't think she want to go."

"She's a child, and she needs to learn what growing up means. And if you're smart, you'll punish *your* daughter the way we all agreed on the plane that they should be punished."

"I change my mind," Jiro said.

Mr. Bronson grabbed Maddie's wrist and started trying to pull her into the rental car.

"No!" she said, and started crying. "No!" She kicked him. We all stared. My mouth fell open.

"You kicked me," her father said. He must have been as shocked as I was.

Jiro spoke more passionately than I'd ever heard him. He said, "Think, think, think. Maddie in danger at your house. She run away again, might get hurt." He looked squarely at Mr. Bronson. "Think about how much danger she in if she run away again. She *will* run away again. These girls need one another."

Mr. Bronson looked genuinely hurt. "My other kids turned out fine."

Jiro said, "Your other kids not Maddie. Maddie spend her life with sisters." Then he turned to us girls. "If your mother want, I stay with you four in Chicago. Maybe Chicago needs some of my gum. If I need to take trip once in a while back to Arkansas, maybe Mack stay with you."

Mack said, "You're going to leave *me* with them?"

Larry, who'd been silently nodding for the past few moments, said, "They're not bad girls. They just want to be together." He looked at the mountains in the distance, then back at us. "I know how it is to want to be with someone and you can't."

I knew he was talking about our mother.

"I'm suing Helen for custody," Mr. Bronson said, his nostrils flaring again.

Larry said, "Good luck with that. In the mean-time, I'm going to talk with Helen about what she wants to do."

"Life ain't a democracy," Mack said. "But I'll agree

to that if it keeps me from having to come all the way out to Colorado again. I got better things to do."

"I strenuously object to my daughter returning to Chicago," Mr. Bronson said.

I said, "You don't have custody, my mother does. Once the judge learns you spank Maddie for wetting her bed, I bet you'll never get custody. I vote for my father's idea."

"What?" Mack cried. "You girls don't get a vote."

"All four of you girls need to be disciplined!" Mr. Bronson said. "That's the trouble. Their mother never disciplines. . . ."

"Hmmm, you not thinking," said Jiro. "Maddie can get hurt if she ran away again. She too sad. Sad about mother. Sad about sisters. You make her too sad."

Again Mr. Bronson looked genuinely hurt. I almost felt sorry for him.

"I agree they should be grounded," Larry said. He held Lakey to him. "It's been great having you. But you belong with your sisters, I understand that now."

I looked at Jiro. "Thanks."

"You did bad thing, but I proud of you," he said.

"Me too. I mean, I'm proud of you."

And I meant it.

chapter eighteen

MADDIE, JIRO, MR. BRONSON, AND I took the rental car together. I couldn't read what Maddie was thinking. I don't think she believed yet that we would all stay at home with Jiro. Then I thought to ask Jiro, "How is Mom?"

"Getting better. Antibiotics work."

They let Maddie and me sit next to each other on the plane while Jiro and Mr. Bronson sat across the aisle. Mr. Bronson barely spoke the rest of the way home, even though Maddie and I giggled loudly and sang songs. I kept waiting for him to tell us to quiet down, but he never did. Though, at one point, when a toddler started crying, Mr. Bronson leaned forward and told the mother, "Parenting is all about discipline." Then he must have noticed a stewardess struggling with an overhead bin. He called out to her, "You need to push that big black one sideways." She ignored him. That actually made me feel a bit bad for him. There he was, thinking he knew everything in the world, and nobody wanted his advice. Several times I saw him gazing sadly out the window at the empty night sky. And I realized suddenly that there was one thing my father, Mr. Bronson, and Mack had in common: They were all outsiders, just like my mother was. And they were all lonely.

Jiro did stay with us in Chicago until my mother had her final surgery a few months later. Often he took us to the hospital instead of Mack. At first this annoyed Mack, but eventually Jiro and Mack actually grew to like each other. One day Mack suddenly slapped Jiro on the shoulder and said, "I love the Japanese. They're fine people."

My sisters really started to bond with Jiro. In fact, Maddie began following him around like he was a guru. Meanwhile, his chocolate gum was a failure, but he found several new customers in Chicago for his regular Gum-Bo, so actually all was well on the gum front.

Then, when it was time for me to visit Jiro for the

Christmas break, all my sisters decided to visit him as well. He met the four of us at an airport in Oklahoma and drove us through the Ozarks.

I said to my sisters, "This is a bunch of plateaus, not hills."

"Why?" Maddie said.

"Because a mountain is where the ground rises because of geological forces that force the ground up into mountains. And the Ozarks are the result of these forces that force . . . anyway, forces that make a plateau."

"Why?"

"Because the earth is alive and constantly moving and full of forces that are constantly forcing the landscape to change."

"Why?"

"Because the earth changes just like we change."

"Why?"

"I don't know. That's what Dad says."

"Why?"

"Because he likes to teach me things."

"Why?"

"Because he's my dad! I quit."

"Why?"

"I quit!"

"Why?!"

"Because I'm tired of Why?"

"Okay," she said, and snuggled into me.

Jiro smiled at me. "You never call me Dad before."

The Ozarks were deserted. All of a sudden Jiro—Dad—said, "Look at this." He turned off his lights, put the car in neutral, and floated downhill as if we were on a river. Nobody talked. I leaned my head out the window, the frigid breeze blowing hair off my face. We swooped down into the valley below.

Maddie had fallen asleep by the time we reached Jiro's house. Jiro carried her inside and laid her on my bed. I just sat next to her and watched her beautiful face as she slept.

On Christmas we four walked along the Gloomy River, and at night we sat with Jiro on the porch with a couple of space heaters. I watched the red glow of the heaters and felt the warmth comfort my cheeks. The trees across the road were bare, cracking the sky with their shadows. My mother was in Paris with her new boyfriend, Dr. Jefferson. A year ago, I wouldn't have believed it if somebody told me my sisters and I would be gathered on the front porch with my father on Christmas Day. But here we were.

I don't know why, but I asked Jiro what his brothers and sister were like. He said, "One happy, one sad, and one in between. I don't know why it happen that way."

"And what about you?" I asked.

"Hmmm," he said. "When you here, I'm happy; when not, I'm lonely."

"Do you miss me, too?" Maddie said.

"You too," he said. At around nine p.m. he went in to bed, leaving us girls to talk.

"What if there's an earthquake?" Maddie said. "Jiro said there are earthquakes sometimes in Arkansas."

"I think that's only in northeastern Arkansas," I said. "At least, I think so."

"What are we going to do tomorrow?"

"I guess the same thing we did today," I said. "That's the way it is in Arkansas. Sometimes you do the same thing every day."

"Okay. Can we bring Goat?"

"We can try."

Anyway, we passed the next two weeks doing pretty much the same thing every day, walking in our boots with my goat along the river for an hour before coming home for dinner. I never would have thought doing the same thing every day could be so much fun. It made me think maybe growing up was a pretty good thing. I could just do the same thing every day and love it.

After our visit we flew back to Chicago. We had to catch a taxi home from the airport. Our mother, back from Paris, was busy. Even with her scars, she was still beautiful, just not perfect. And as soon as she was able, she'd gone right back to the universe where beauty meant everything. But I noticed that even Dr. Jefferson had a sad quality about him. Maybe he was lonely, too. I wished I could change her, but I couldn't. I couldn't bring her happiness the way I could with Jiro.

I would never be truly lonely as long as my sisters were okay. The line between loneliness and happiness seemed slender to me. If I were killed by a car tomorrow, Jiro would be unhappy. If anything happened to any of my sisters, I would be unhappy. You were taking a chance by letting someone make you happy or sad. My mother had never wanted to take that chance, for whatever reason. Those were some pretty big thoughts I had, if I say so myself.

READING GROUP GUIDE

Discussion Questions

1) Exploring the bonds that bind a family is one of the major themes of the story. What are some of the expressions of closeness that the sisters display?

2) What are some of the characteristics the sisters share? What are some of their differences?

3) What adjectives would you use to describe Shelby? Marilyn? Lakey? Maddie? Helen?

4) The impact of Helen's behavior on the sisters is complex. How does her attitude toward men shape the sisters' attitudes? How does her use of her beauty affect them?

5) How do the sisters view their mom's beauty? How do they reflect her values?

6) In many families the siblings take care of one another. Describe the relationship of Shelby and

Maddie before they go to live with their fathers and then while they are separated.

7) How do the fathers relate to Helen now that they are no longer with her? How do they relate to their daughters? How do they relate to one another?

8) The discussion of marriage comes up many times in the story. How has their mother's desire not to marry affected the sisters?

9) Helen and the fathers are described as outsiders. Helen found each man through their shared loneliness. Have the sisters also become outsiders? Can they change?

10) Which sister is the most rebellious? Who is the most compliant? Who is the most motherly? Give examples that support your choices.

11) We learn both from our parents and from our surroundings. Do the characters in this book reflect both parental and environmental influences? Give examples of what the sisters have learned from their parents. Now give examples of things they have

learned from their surroundings. List some of the things the sisters have experienced because of their unusual lifestyle.

12) The isolation that the sisters felt when they were sent to their fathers' houses was both geographical and personal. With the technology available today, including cell phones, camera phones, and the Internet and its social networking sites, how might the girls' situation be altered?

13) How did the powwow process help the sisters communicate? Did this always work for them?

14) How does each sister view her mother? Her father? Herself?

15) What personality characteristics do the girls share with their fathers? How were Mack and Marilyn similar? Lakey and Larry? Shelby and Jiro? Maddie and Mr. Bronson?

16) By the end of the book, which character has changed the most in this story? Has any character remained unchanged?

Research and Activities

1) Did you understand the special language, Thethe-guh, that the sisters speak (page 25)? Try writing a sentence using their special language. Have you ever made up your own language? Try making one up.

2) Diagram on paper the complex family tree of Shelby and her sisters. Include Helen, as well as all of the fathers, sisters, and any other brothers and sisters and spouses. How does this compare to a traditional family tree?

3) Get a map of the United States and chart the places mentioned in the story as the girls travel with their mom, when they are with their dads, and when they run away. Where do they eventually end up?

4) Each of the girls has a distinct look they feel helps define them. Using magazines, can you find pictures that you think show characteristics of a Japanese girl? A Japanese-Italian girl? A Japanese-Anglo girl? Put these pictures together to create their family. How significant is physical appearance in the bond of families?

When the North Vietnamese attack a Dega village immediately after the Vietnam War, Tin and his elephant escape into the depths of the jungle. Join Newbery Medal–winning author Cynthia Kadohata as she explores a world both heartbreaking and full of hope.

Turn the page for an excerpt from

A Million Shades of Gray

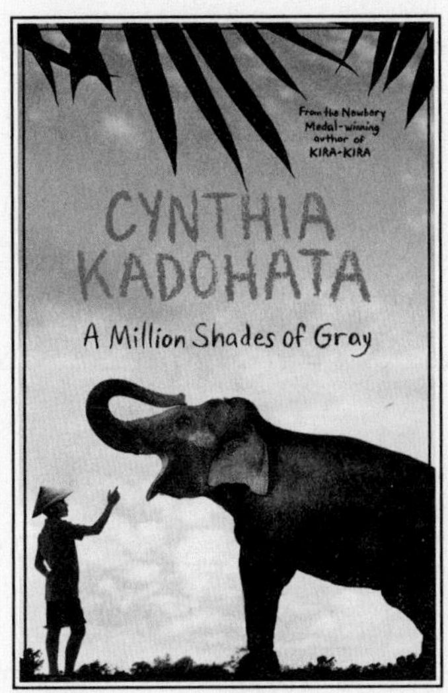

AVAILABLE JANUARY 2010 FROM

ATHENEUM BOOKS FOR YOUNG READERS

"Lady, *nao*," Tomas said, and she calmly followed him, dragging the three huge logs behind her.

Y'Tin felt a rush of happiness. When they reached the gate to the village, he sat up with his chest sticking out proudly. Lady followed Tomas to the site where the new longhouse would be built. The Buonyas were one of the biggest clans in the village, so they were planning a house that would be one hundred meters long. That translated to a lot of logs.

And so it went for the rest of the afternoon, with Lady and Y'Tin going back and forth from the jungle to the site. At one point Lady actually kneeled when he told her to. It was just about the best day of Y'Tin's life.

That night, as he lay in his family's room in the clan's longhouse, the others slept while he stayed up going over and over the whole afternoon. He could see Lady clearly when he closed his eyes. He felt giddy. Everyone kept saying that he was too young to know what his future held, but he knew as well as he knew anything that he would spend his life as an elephant handler. Still, his father had told him to always think about "the other hand." So, on the other hand, he had been working with Lady for many months now,

1973, Central Highlands, South Vietnam

Y'Tin Eban watched Tomas fasten the rope around Lady's neck. Lady was the smallest of the village's three elephants, but she was also the strongest, so she was much in demand as a worker. Today Lady would be dragging logs for the Buonya clan. The Buonya's house had caught fire and they were building a new one.

Y'Tin stood behind and to the side of Tomas. Sometimes Tomas got annoyed by how closely Y'Tin stood, but Y'Tin didn't want to miss anything. On the other hand, Y'Tin didn't want to annoy Tomas too much, or he might refuse to train Tin further. At fourteen, Tomas Knul was the youngest elephant handler ever in the village, but Y'Tin hoped to beat that record. Y'Tin was only eleven, but he was confident that he would someday be a fine elephant handler.

"Stand back," Tomas snapped. "Or I won't let you work with the elephants today."

Y'Tin dutifully stepped back. He did whatever Tomas told him to do. There were other kids who hung around the elephants, but Y'Tin was the one Tomas had chosen to train. Tomas had assured him that when the time was right, Y'Tin would become Lady's handler. Y'Tin didn't want him to change his mind.

One of the kids who hung around got too close, and Y'Tin snapped, "Stand back," just as Tomas had snapped to him.

Tomas glanced at Y'Tin. "I was thinking I'd let you ride her into the village today. I'll walk beside you. Do you think you're ready?"

"I'm ready," Y'Tin said. He had been ready for months. He patted Lady's side; she ignored him.

Tomas looked at him thoughtfully. "I think you want to be an elephant handler even more than I once did."

"Sure thing," Y'Tin said in English. He had learned that from one of the American Special Forces soldiers his father knew. The Americans had many words for "yes." "Sure," "okay," "right," "affirmative," "absolutely," "yeah," "check," "Roger that," and "Sure do, tennis shoe" immediately came to mind.

Y'Tin walked around to Lady's trunk to have a talk with her. "I'm going to ride you in today, Lady. You need to behave yourself."

As if in answer, Lady pushed Y'Tin to the ground—and she didn't let him up. It was embarrassing. He tried to get away, but Lady was too strong. "Tomas," he said. "Uh, can you help me?"

Tomas rolled his eyes. "Lady!" he said sharply, and Lady let Y'Tin up. "You've got to be firmer with her," Tomas scolded Y'Tin. "Use your hook to keep her in line."

"But I want her to like me."

"You want her to respect you. Now help get those logs attached to her rope." Y'Tin and one of the Buonya boys tied huge logs to the end of the rope attached to Lady's harness. She would haul the logs to the building site.

When the logs were secure, Y'Tin said, "*Muk*, Lady." But she refused to kneel. "*Muk!*" He noticed Tomas looking at him. "*Muk!*" he said again. Y'Tin could feel his face growing hot. He took his stick with the hook and poked her with it. She still didn't respond.

"Lady, *muk*," Tomas said mildly, and she immediately kneeled.

Y'Tin climbed aboard her, his legs straddling her back. "Lady, up," Y'Tin commanded, and for once she listened.

and he didn't seem to be making much headway with her. When she kneeled and stood up on command today was the first time she had ever listened to him.

Tomas always warned him not to become too friendly with her or she wouldn't respect him. He liked to remind Y'Tin of the time a few years ago when Lady went into a rage for some mysterious reason. Y'Tin still remembered the huge gap in the fence that she had stampeded.

Y'Tin's father was sleeping fitfully, mumbling about the Americans. His father had a lot on his mind lately. He worked with the American Special Forces, and had been talking to Y'Tin's mother about the possibility of becoming a Christian. He hadn't made any decisions about it yet. He often took a long time to make a decision. For instance, it had taken him close to two years to allow Y'Tin to work with the elephants, and it had taken him a year to decide to work with the Americans.

So far the remoteness of the village had saved it from the worst of what the Americans called the Vietnam War and what his father called the American War. Y'Tin hoped the war would be over by the time he was grown. North and South Vietnam had been fighting since well before Y'Tin was born. The Americans fought with the South.

All his father thought about was the war, and all Y'Tin thought about was elephants. Y'Tin knew he was different from the other boys in that he did not want to be a farmer. That's why his parents worried about him so much. There was just one thing he wanted: to be an elephant handler. Meanwhile, Y'Tin did so poorly in school, his parents were disappointed in him. His older sister, H'Juaih, got the highest marks. He was proud of her, but that didn't mean he wanted to be like her.

"Y'Tin?" his mother called out from the darkness.

"Yes, Ami."

"I knew you were still awake."

And, indeed, she often did know when he was awake, although he didn't make a sound. He never knew whether she was awake or sleeping. Either way, she was silent.

"Are you daydreaming again?"

He didn't answer.

"If you spent as much time on your homework as you do on your daydreaming, your grades would be the same as H'Juaih's."

"Ami, I was just thinking. That's different from daydreaming."

"Daydreaming is thinking about things that aren't true yet. Thinking is when you ponder matters that are already true."

She didn't answer, and he knew he had won the argument. On the other hand, maybe she just stopped talking because she was tired. He was tired also. He closed his eyes and watched Lady until he fell asleep.

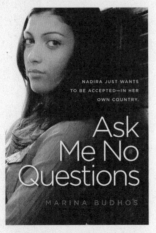

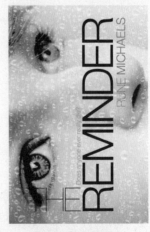

Read all the NEWBERY MEDAL Winners from Atheneum!

THE HIGHER POWER OF LUCKY
by Susan Patron

KIRA-KIRA
by Cynthia Kadohata

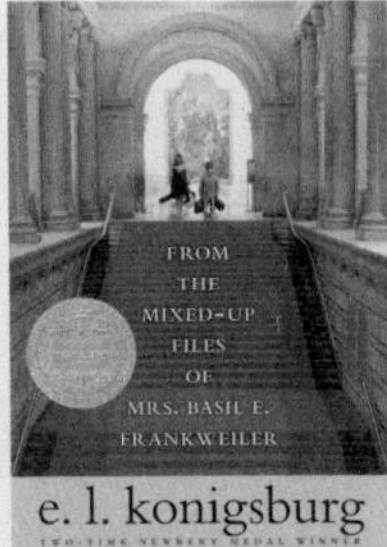

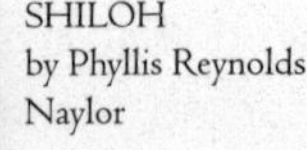

SHILOH
by Phyllis Reynolds Naylor

DICEY'S SONG
by Cynthia Voigt

FROM THE MIXED-UP FILES OF MRS. BASIL E. FRANKWEILER
by E. L. Konigsburg

THE VIEW FROM SATURDAY
by E. L. Konigsburg

MRS. FRISBY AND THE RATS OF NIMH
by Robert C. O'Brien

THE SLAVE DANCER
by Paula Fox

PUBLISHED BY SIMON & SCHUSTER